英漢對照

第二版

莎士比亞十四行詩集
Shakespeare's Sonnets

William Shakespeare◎著

辜正坤◎譯

台灣大學外文系
彭鏡禧教授◎專文推薦

英漢對照

第二版

莎士比亞十四行詩集
Shakespeare's Sonnets

國家圖書館出版品預行編目資料

莎士比亞十四行詩集 /
William Shakespeare 作；辜正坤譯.
-- 二版. -- 臺北市：書林
2025.03　面；　公分
譯自：Shakespeare's sonnets
ISBN 978-626-7605-09-7(平裝)

873.43384　　　　　　　　　114000472

世界詩選 18
莎士比亞十四行詩集（第二版）
Shakespeare's Sonnets 2nd Edition

作　　　者	William Shakespeare
譯　　　者	辜正坤
編　　　輯	陳衍秀、劉純瑀
出　版　者	書林出版有限公司
	100 台北市羅斯福路四段 60 號 3 樓
	Tel (02) 2368-4938・2365-8617 Fax (02) 2368-8929・2363-6630
台北書林書店	106 台北市新生南路三段 88 號 2 樓之 5　Tel (02) 2365-8617
學校業務部	Tel (02) 2368-7226・(04) 2376-3799・(07) 229-0300
經銷業務部	Tel (02) 2368-4938
發　行　人	蘇正隆
郵　　　撥	15743873・書林出版有限公司
網　　　址	http://www.bookman.com.tw
登　　　記　證	局版臺業字第一八三一號
出　版　日　期	2006 年一版，2025 年 3 月二版初刷
定　　　價	350 元
I S B N	978-626-7605-09-7

欲利用本書全部或部分內容者，須徵得書林出版有限公司同意或書面授權。請洽書林出版部，Tel (02) 2368-4938。

Chinese translation, notes, and introduction by Zhengkun Gu
Copyright ©2006 by Bookman Books, Ltd. All rights reserved.

William Shakespeare，1564-1616

Elizabeth I of England，1533-1603

Henry Wriothesley, 3rd Earl of Southampton,1573-1624
Shakespeare's patron at twenty-one years of age

Shakespeare's Sonnets

Contents

Foreword by Ching-hsi Perng   1

Introduction   5

On the Translation of Shakespeare's Sonnets   9

Shakespeare's Sonnets   16

Lection   324

Glossary   329

Best Links   344

莎士比亞十四行詩集

目　　錄

序：新聲與新貌／彭鏡禧教授　　1

導讀　　5

莎士比亞十四行詩的翻譯　　9

莎士比亞十四行詩　　16

異文　　324

莎士比亞十四行詩用語辭典　　329

好站連結　　344

莎士比亞十四行詩集

新聲與新貌：
序辜譯《莎士比亞十四行詩集》

彭鏡禧
臺灣大學外國語文學系及戲劇學系教授

　　莎士比亞的十四行詩最大的成就在於「以流利自然的語調，表現出多樣而複雜的心緒。」精研莎學的美國學者 Stephen Booth 認為「……莎士比亞遣詞用字的適切意義與其前後文意互相聯結、糾纏、糅合、衝突，造成足以令人目眩的複雜性，而讀者自其中感到率真純樸。」正是這種複雜性，賦予了這些詩篇所謂的「十四行詩的魔術」——舉重若輕，馭繁如簡。[1]

　　這樣的作品形成了文學翻譯者嚴峻的挑戰，但是歷來接受挑戰的翻譯家不乏其人；筆者為文討論過的莎士比亞十四行詩中文全譯本就多達七種。[2]各家譯者對原詩的領受各有不同，對譯事的見解各有堅持。這些見解和領受，表現在他們對原作的音韻節奏、字詞順序、修辭特色、多義性等文學特質的處理方式，因為這些恰是「莎

---

[1] 原文見 Stephen Booth, ed., Shakespeare's Sonnets. New Haven and London: Yale UP, 1979. xiii. 參見拙文〈撒謊的詩人（？）——論莎士比亞《十四行詩》的中譯〉，原刊《中外文學》12.11（1984年4月）：108-36；收入拙著《細說莎士比亞：論文集》（臺北：國立臺灣大學出版中心，民國九十三年）331。

[2] 譯者分別是虞爾昌、屠岸、梁實秋、施穎洲、梁宗岱、楊耐東以及陳次雲。

翁原作的魔力所在」。③

　　1998年我參加北京大學舉行的翻譯學術研討會，有幸結識辜正坤教授，獲贈他剛出版的這個譯本，並得以聆聽他對英詩中譯的高見，覺得頗有新意。簡單的說，他認爲莎翁 abab cdcd efef gg 的「多元韻式」並不符合中國讀者對音韻美的感覺，「總使讀者覺得自己好像在閱讀散文似的，雖也算得一種風格，卻不如一元韻式音調鏗鏘。」因此他「採用了符合傳統中國詩中較通行的一韻到底的韻式」，以求「流暢、中聽」。④這和以往譯本力求追隨莎翁原詩多元韻式（同時也是開放韻式）的方向，可謂大相逕庭。

　　一旦韻腳鬆了綁，譯文自然就可以更加活潑自由；也可以說，爲了儘量達到一韻到底，有時必須稍微更動原詩的意思——就如爲了保持原詩的多元韻式，許多譯者也必須更動原意或詩行或意象。正因爲一元韻式是中國詩歌的主流，譯文要達到最佳效果，尤須有深厚的國學根柢，才有可能使莎士比亞眞正入籍中華。辜教授以他對原詩精當的理解，以及對中文準確的掌握，成品斐然成章，流暢可誦。其中最精彩的，莫過於第66首：

　　　　難耐不平事，何如悄然去泉臺：
　　　　休說是天才，偏生作乞丐，
　　　　人道是草包，偏把金銀戴，
　　　　說什麼信與義，眼見無人睬，

---

③ 詳見《細說莎士比亞》329-65。
④ 辜正坤，〈關於莎士比亞十四行詩的翻譯問題〉。辜正坤譯，《莎士比亞十四行詩集》（北京：北京大學出版社，1998）7。

莎士比亞十四行詩集

　　道什麼榮與辱，全是瞎安排，
　　少女童貞可憐遭橫暴，
　　堂堂正義無端受掩埋，
　　跛腿權勢反弄殘了擂台漢，
　　墨客騷人官府門前口難開，
　　蠢驢們偏掛著指迷釋惑教授招牌，
　　多少真話錯喚作愚魯癡呆，
　　善惡易位，小人反受大人拜。
　　　　不平，難耐，索不如一死化纖埃，
　　　　待去也，又怎好讓愛人獨守空階？

　　原詩十四行當中，有十行用 And 起首，第一行和第十三行又都用 Tired with all these 起首；如此大量使用修辭學中的首詞重複法 (anaphora)，令人讀來格外有人生乏味、可厭之感。前人的翻譯對此一修辭法多半束手，辜譯則利用相似詞義或相似語法以為彌補，效果良好，而用韻、遣詞、節奏頗有舊詞曲的韻味，更是成功的關鍵。討論翻譯，近有所謂「歸化法」和「異化法」之說。辜譯可以畫入前者。

　　西洋十四行詩始於義大利，最常見的結構是前八行，後六行；韻腳方面，前八行是 abba abba，後六行則為 cdecde 或 cdcdcd。相較之下，莎士比亞多用了二至三個韻，這是因為「義大利文韻母較少，而同韻字較多……；英文韻母較多，同韻字較少。」[5]詩人為

---

[5] 夏燕生，〈十四行詩及其受宮廷愛情詩的影響〉。齊邦媛編輯，《西洋詩歌研究》（台北：中央文物供應社，民國七十五年）192。

003

Shakespeare's Sonnets

了配合本國語言特色而挪用外國詩體裁，以免削足適履，乃是理所當然。否則「莎式十四行詩」也不會成爲「英式十四行詩」的同義詞了。翻譯家爲了拓寬本國文學的領域，固然可以追求原作的形與義，但像辜教授的作法，放棄一部份的形，由新聲產生新貌，使譯文更貼近本國文，應該也是一個可以努力的方向。

導讀：莎士比亞十四行詩

辜正坤

一、背景

莎士比亞十四行詩大約創作於 1590 年至 1598 年之間，1609 年初版，由倫敦的出版商托馬斯・索普(Thomas Thorpe, 1570-1635?)獨家印行，收詩 154 首，是莎詩集最早、最完全的「第一四開本」(Quarto)。[1]（1640 年，又出了一個本森(John Benson)的新版本，少收了 8 首，詩的順序亦做了若干更動。十七世紀，沒有出現過其他版本。《莎士比亞十四行詩集》在莎學界引起巨大的興趣和爭論，有關它的許多謎至今未曾解開。

比較流行的看法是從第 1 首到第 126 首，是詩人寫給他的男友，一位俊俏的貴族青年的；從第 127 首到第 152 首，是寫給一位黑膚女郎的；最後兩首及中間個別幾首與故事無關。「朋友說」和「黑女郎說」是英國莎學家馬隆(Edmond Malone, 1741-1812)和斯帝文斯(George Steevens, 1736-1800)在 1780 年提出的。在此之前，人們相信這些詩大部分或全部都是歌頌愛人的。然而「朋友說」雖流

---

[1] 編註：莎士比亞早期出版的作品依裝幀尺寸不同，分別稱為「對開本」(Folio)與「四開本」(Quarto)。對開本的尺寸約為 30×22 公分，四開本的尺寸約為 16×12 公分。Thomas Thorpe 於 1609 年印行的莎士比亞十四行詩「第一四開本」(The First Quarto)，歷經各家修訂，仍為當代通行之各種莎詩版本的依據。

行極廣，反對者也大有人在。如十九世紀初的英國詩人兼莎評家柯立芝(Samuel Taylor Coleridge, 1772-1834)就堅持，莎氏十四行詩全部都是呈獻給作者所愛的一個女人的。根據我個人多年的研究，我的結論是：
1. 莎士比亞十四行詩大部分是獻給女性的，但不止一位女性。
2. 其中的一位女性不是別人，正是那位赫赫有名的伊莉莎白女王(Elizabeth I of England, 1533-1603)。
3. 剩下的一小部分則是獻給兩位男朋友的，一位是伊莉莎白女王的老臣艾塞克斯伯爵(Robert Devereux, 2nd Earl of Essex, 1566-1601)，另一位是艾塞克斯的心腹（也是莎士比亞的庇護人）南安普敦伯爵(Henry Wriothesley, 3rd Earl of Southampton, 1573-1624)。

二、主題與內容

綜觀154首十四行詩，主題不外描寫時間、友誼、愛情、詩藝。往往若干首成一詩組，表現同一題材。粗讀之下，難免給人一種重複感，似乎是詩人隨心所欲的練筆之作。但因為詩本身的結構技巧和語言技巧都很高，所以幾乎每首詩都有獨立存在的審美價值。

從詩中的描寫的確可以窺見詩人靈魂深處的東西，其人格無異是被徹底地曝了一次光，這些詩使我們感到，詩人同我們一樣是實實在在的人，充滿了激情與苦惱。一方面表現為對善的執著，對惡的鞭撻，對愛情和友誼的憧憬與追求；另一方面又表現為對現實的不滿，對理想破滅的厭恨，對道德負罪感的反抗。透過那些閃閃爍爍

爍，或真誠或虛飾的詩行，我們感到詩人人格的各方面——崇高與卑劣，偉大與渺小，自矜與自卑——都突顯在詩的屏幕上。我們可以感受到，在全部詩中占統治地位的，歸根結底是一個「愛」字（第 105 首）。在否定中世紀黑暗時代的禁欲主義和神權的基礎上，人文主義讚揚人的個性，宣稱人生而平等，賦予了人類生存的重要性和新的意義。莎詩處處浸透了這種精神，處處充滿對生活的歌頌和懷疑，對人的本質的歌頌與懷疑，對自我的歌頌與懷疑。在第 105 首詩中，詩人宣稱，他的詩將永遠歌頌真、善、美，永遠歌頌這三者合一的化身——他的愛人，這實際上等於說，他所歌頌的最高目標就是愛，而真、善、美最終統一在愛裡。

三、十四行詩體

　　十四行詩(Sonnet)這種藝術形式在莎士比亞手中得到了新的發展。十四行詩體起源於義大利。佩脫拉克(Petrarch, 1304-1374)是最早著名的十四行詩作者。他的十四行詩，由一組八行詩(Octave)和一組六行詩(Sestet)構成，八行詩的韻式為 abba abba，六行詩的韻式則有下列三種：(1)cdecde (2)cdcdcd (3)cdedce。十六世紀初葉，英國貴族薩瑞伯爵亨利・霍沃德(Henry Howard, Earl of Surrey, 1517-1547)和托馬斯・魏阿特爵士(Sir Thomas Wyatt, 1503-1542)把這種詩體移植到英國後，形式略有變化。莎氏十四行詩體的韻式同於薩瑞伯爵的第一種韻式：abab cdcd efef gg。後來此式逐稱為「莎士比亞式」或「英國式」。莎士比亞在運用這個詩體時，極為得心應手。主要表現為語彙豐富，用詞洗鍊，比喻新穎，結構巧妙，音調鏗鏘悅耳。

而他最擅長的是最後兩行詩，往往構思奇詭，語出驚人，既是全詩點睛之作，又自成一聯警語格言。如第 2 首：「如此，你縱然已衰老，美卻會重生，／你縱然血已冰涼，也自會借體重溫。」第 11 首：「她刻你是要把你作爲一枚圓章，／多多蓋印，豈可讓圓章徒有虛名！」第 28 首：「然而白天卻一天天使我憂心加重，／夜晚則一晚晚使我愁思更濃。」第 29 首：「但記住你柔情招來財無限，／縱帝王屈尊就我，不與換江山。」第 74 首：「我這微軀所值全賴有內在之魂，／忠魂化詩句，長伴你度過餘生。」第 87 首：「好一場春夢裡與你情深意濃，／夢裡王位在，醒覺萬事空。」第 135 首：「別，別無情拒絕求愛的風流種，／想萬欲無非是欲，我的欲有甚不同？」

　　十四行詩在十六世紀的英國曾盛極一時，名家輩出，除上述的薩瑞、魏阿特之外，錫得尼(Philip Sidney, 1554-1586)、斯本塞(Edmund Spencer, 1552-1599)、但尼爾(Samuel Daniel, 1562-1619)等人，都獲得了很高的成就。莎士比亞之後，密爾頓(John Milton, 1608-1674)、華茲華斯(William Wordsworth, 1770-1850)、雪萊(Percy Bysshe Shelley, 1792-1822)、濟慈(John Keats, 1795-1821)、勃朗寧夫人(Elizabeth Browning, 1806-1861)，奧頓(W. H Auden, 1907-1973)等算得上是後起之秀。但是，在整個英國十四行詩乃至於世界十四行詩的創作中，莎士比亞的十四行詩是一座高峰，當得起空前絕後的美稱。

莎士比亞十四行詩集

莎士比亞十四行詩的翻譯

一、譯詩的三個問題

　　翻譯莎士比亞十四行詩有幾點值得討論。第一，莎士比亞十四行詩措辭通常十分華麗，所以譯詩也須相應華麗，才能與原作辭氣相合。如果譯得太質，雖也算一種風格，終究有背原作詩風。如果譯得太古奧，在當今白話盛行的時代，顯然是不適宜的。我的作法是不譯成古體詩，但注重詞彙用語須雅致，與白話保持適當的距離。第二，莎士比亞在十四行詩中喜用雙關語，尤其是有關性方面的雙關語，這是翻譯中最難的部分。如果不反映出莎士比亞十四行詩的這個特點，那麼無疑是在一定的程度上歪曲了莎士比亞，同時從這一特點也可以看出伊莉莎白時代的某種世俗風氣；但如果過分渲染了莎詩的這一特點，則對於普通中國人來說，又未免有傷風化。所以我總是很小心地對待這個問題，儘量用比較隱晦的雙關語來模擬傳達莎士比亞十四行詩中的性暗示，同時也考慮到中國人的接受能力。第三，莎士比亞十四行詩的韻式是比較嚴格的，基本上採用 ababcdcdefefgg 形式。在翻譯的時候是否也採用這個韻式？我的回答是，可以用原詩的韻式譯，也可以用符合中國人審美習慣的韻式來譯。現行已有的譯本，多半都是力圖仿照原詩韻式來譯的，這種作法的意圖固然很好，但是否是英詩漢譯的唯一模式或最佳模式，還有待進一步探討。由於詩歌的

音美在大多數的情況下屬於不可譯因素，所以我以爲也可以不照搬原詩的韻式，不妨在講明原詩韻式的情況下，用中國詩的韻式來創造一種音美，力求譯詩音美效果的強烈程度能和原詩接近。

二、譯詩的三種流派

外國詩一般間行押韻（可稱爲「多元韻式」），取 ababcdcd 形式較多；而中國詩取 aaba 形式較多（即第二、四、六行一定押韻，且往往是同一個韻，可稱爲「一元韻式」）。翻譯的時候，譯者往往分爲三派，一是完全按照原詩的形式間行押韻，一派是略作修正，按中國的方式押韻，一派是根本不押韻。應該說三派各有好處。第一派的好處在於尊重了原詩間行押韻的特點，在音美方面照顧了原詩，其弊則在於此種韻脚不爲傳統的中國讀者所熟悉，他們讀這樣的譯詩只感到形式特別，卻難以覺得韻律美。第二派的好處在於尊重中國詩的傳統，照顧了中國讀者的審美習慣，所以往往能在音美方面獲得成功。其弊則在於未完全按原詩的格式押韻，在音似意義上降低了近似度。第三派由於不受韻律的限制，在遣詞造句方面可以自由些，故在內容方面較其他兩派更容易近似於原作，其弊在於缺乏音美。現舉莎翁十四行詩第 97 首譯文兩種作爲第一派和第二派譯法的例證：

第 97 首

與君別離後，多像是過冬天，
你是時光流轉中惟一的歡樂！

我覺得好冷,日子好黑暗!
好一派歲暮荒寒的景色!
這離別其實是在夏天;
凸了肚皮的豐盛的秋季
承受著春天縱樂的負擔,
像丈夫死後遺在腹內的子息:
不過對於我,這子孫的繁衍
只是生一個無父孤兒的指望;
因為夏天的歡樂都在你的身畔,
你一去,鳥兒都停了歌唱:
　　即使歌唱,也是無精打采,
　　使得樹葉變色,生怕冬天要來。
　　　　　　　　(梁實秋譯)

第97首

你是這飛逝年華中的快樂與期盼,
一旦離開了你,日子便宛若冬寒。
瑟縮的冰冷攫住了我,天色多麼陰暗!
四望一片蕭疏,滿目是歲末的凋殘。
可是這離別的日子分明是在夏日,
或孕育著富饒充實的秋天,
浪蕩春情已經結下瑩瑩碩果,
好像良人的遺孀,胎動小腹圓。

Shakespeare's Sonnets

　　然而這豐盈的果實在我眼中，
　　只是亡人的孤兒，無父的遺產。
　　夏天和夏天之樂都聽你支配，
　　你一旦離去，連小鳥也緘口不言。
　　　它們即便啟開歌喉，只吐出聲聲哀怨，
　　　使綠葉疑隆冬將至，愁色罩蒼顏。

（辜正坤譯）

　　從譯詩中可以看出，梁譯屬於第一派譯風，想用 abab cdcd efef gg 的韻式譯，除了第一、三行與第九、十一行在押韻上重複之外，其餘均間行押韻，力摹莎氏原詩的押韻格式。梁譯在這個方面基本上是成功的。但如果為中國讀者著想，則詩的押韻在音美方面就未必美了。讀者習慣了傳統的中國一元韻式，難以從英詩的二元韻式中得到美感。在漢詩中，當「明月出天山」一出現，我們往往本能記住「山」是 an「安」韻，因此，當「蒼茫雲海間」的「間」字一出現時，正和我們的心理期待相同，我們有一種很舒服的感覺，並期待在第四行重新碰到這個 an 音。所以當「長風幾萬里／吹度玉門關」的「關」字一出現時，人人覺胸腔裡無處不熨貼，無處不舒服。可是讀梁譯時，由於第一行是「想」結尾，第二行是「我」結尾，是二元韻式，讀者不習慣把兩種發音都同時記住，頂多記住「想」「方」的韻腳效果（ang「昂」韻），可是剛記住這點，下面又換了韻，讀者完全給弄糊塗了，他得另起爐灶，培養起新的韻腳感，並且仍然是二重的！由於絕大多數中國讀者沒有這種審美心理習

慣,所以這種韻式在取得譯詩的音美方面難以成功。但這種譯法本身也是有功勞的,因為,這為中國讀者在一定的程度上顯示出莎翁十四行詩原有的押韻格式。

　　辜譯則屬於第二派譯風,由於採用了符合傳統中國詩中較通行的一韻到底的韻式,故顯得流暢、中聽一些。這種韻似乎行行都在提醒讀者:這是詩。當然,辜譯亦有弊:即未傳達莎詩原有韻式。利弊相較,我以為多元韻式(間行韻,如梁譯)總使讀者覺得自己好像在閱讀散文似的,雖也算得一種風格,卻不如一元韻式音調鏗鏘,所以其音美效果在漢譯中不太理想。當然,梁譯法和辜譯法對於詩歌翻譯均有利弊,可以互補生輝,不必獨尊一家一法。至於第三種譯法,道理十分明白,這裡就不再舉例了。這些譯法與所謂「失之東隅,收之桑榆」的譯法相通,全譯不可能,則取半可譯;半可譯尚不能,就取意譯、神譯、創譯,力爭形有失而援神補,神有虧而圖形勝,自能左右逢源,譯筆生輝。這一點可以參考中外漢詩英譯譯者的作法,他們多半是不太顧及漢詩本身的押韻格式。例如漢詩一韻到底,譯成英語詩後常常根據情況換韻,很少能夠從頭到尾採用一元韻式,尤其是當漢詩比較長時,在英譯詩中要作到一韻到底,基本上不可能。所以,從客觀情況來看,翻譯詩歌時,根據母語的具體條件靈活處理韻式,這是理所當然的事情。

三、結語

　　翻譯莎士比亞十四行詩對筆者來說是一種享受。在翻譯之前，筆者曾閱讀過梁宗岱、屠岸和梁實秋等先生的譯本。梁譯相當嚴謹，規行矩步，儘量扣緊原詩，譯詩是成功的；缺點是過分拘謹，句式較板滯，似乎缺乏莎士比亞原詩那種華美律動的詩風。屠譯在用語通順流暢方面下過很大的工夫，讀起來頗具詩味，也是相當成功的譯本。缺點是莎士比亞原詩的華美風格有所減弱，若干雙關語似乎也故意不加以處理。梁實秋先生的譯本則比前兩者都樸素，開了另一種譯風，加上對詩行中的語言難處有註解，所以既有可讀性，也有學術性。缺點是語風過於淺白，詩味不及前兩者濃。總而言之，這幾個譯本都起過很大的作用，功勞是很大的。拙譯則試圖另闢蹊徑，補苴罅漏，以期讓莎士比亞十四行詩多一種供讀者鑒賞的面目，結果如何，尚待讀者評判。

莎士比亞十四行詩集

　　　　謹致
　　　本集十四行詩之
　　　　惟一促成者
　　　W.H.先生，
　　　祝他洪福齊天
　　　恰如我們不朽之詩人
　　　　筆下所謳
　　　　芳名永在。
　　　　心存善念
　　　　而冒昧
　　　　　付梓
　　　　　　者
　　　　　　　T.T.

Sonnet 1

From fairest creatures we desire increase,
That thereby beauty's rose might never die,
But as the riper should by time decease,
His tender heir might bear his memory;
But thou, contracted to thine own bright eyes,
Feed'st thy light's flame with self-substantial fuel,
Making a famine where abundance lies,
Thyself thy foe, to thy sweet self too cruel.
Thou that art now the world's fresh ornament
And only herald to the gaudy spring
Within thine own bud buriest thy content,
And, tender churl, mak'st waste in niggarding.
Pity the world, or else this glutton be :
To eat the world's due, by the grave and thee.

1

我們總願美的物種繁衍昌盛，
好讓美的玫瑰永遠也不凋零。
縱然時序難逆，物壯必老，
自有年輕的子孫來一脈相承。
而你，卻只與自己的明眸訂婚，
焚身為火，好燒出眼中的光明。①
你與自我為敵，作踐馨香的自身，
有如在豐饒之鄉偏造成滿地饑民。
你是當今世界鮮美的裝飾，
你是錦繡春光裡報春的先行。
你用自己的花苞埋葬自己的花精，
如慷慨的吝嗇者用吝嗇將血本賠盡。
　　可憐這個世界吧，你這貪得無厭之人，
　　不留遺嗣在人間，②只落得蕭條葬孤墳。

---

①伊莉莎白時代的人認為，眼睛同太陽一樣，可放射出光焰。莎詩中有多處提到眼睛時，均寓此義（如第33首第2行）。
②原文是 To eat the world's due，直譯意為「吃掉了人世間（世界）應得的那一份」。「人世間（世界）應得的那一份」指的是人的後代。所以這裡譯作「不留遺嗣在人間」。此句的其他譯法亦可作參考：「就吞噬世界的份」（梁宗岱）；「你吞食了這世界應得的一份」（梁實秋）；「可憐這個世界吧，世界應得的東西/別讓你和墳墓吞吃到一無所遺！」（屠岸）

Sonnet 2

When forty winters shall besiege thy brow
And dig deep trenches in thy beauty's field,
Thy youth's proud livery, so gazed on now,
Will be a totter'd weed, of small worth held.
Then being asked, where all thy beauty lies,
Where all the treasure of thy lusty days,
To say within thine own deep-sunken eyes
Were an all-eating shame and thriftless praise.
How much more praise deserved thy beauty's use
If thou couldst answer 'This fair child of mine
Shall sum my count, and make my old excuse',
Proving his beauty by succession thine.
This were to be new made when thou art old,
And see thy blood warm when thou feel'st it cold.

2

四十個冬天將會圍攻你的額頭,
在你那美麗的田地上掘下淺槽深溝。
那時,你如今令人欽羨的青春華服
將不免價落千丈,寒傖而又鄙陋。
如有人問起,何處尚存你當年的美色,
或何處有遺芳可追尋你往昔的風流,
你卻只能說:「它們都在我深陷的眼裡。」
這回答是空洞的頌揚,徒令答者蒙羞。
但假如你能說:「這裡有我美麗的孩子
可續我韶華春夢,免我老邁時的隱憂」,
那麼孩子之美就是你自身美的明證,
你如這樣使用美,方值得謳頌千秋。

　　如此,你縱然已衰老,美卻會重生,
　　你縱然血已冰涼,也自會借體重溫。

Shakespeare's Sonnets

Sonnet 3

Look in thy glass, and tell the face thou viewest
Now is the time that face should form another,
Whose fresh repair if now thou not renewest
Thou dost beguile the world, unbless some mother.
For where is she so fair whose uneared womb
Disdains the tillage of thy husbandry?
Or who is he so fond will be the tomb
Of his self-love to stop posterity?
Thou art thy mother's glass, and she in thee
Calls back the lovely April of her prime;
So thou through windows of thine age shalt see,
Despite of wrinkles, this thy golden time.
But if thou live remembered not to be,
Die single, and thine image dies with thee.

3

照照鏡子去吧，給鏡中臉兒報一個信，
是時候了，那張臉兒理應來一個再生。
假如你現在不複製下它未褪的風采，
你就騙了這個世界，叫它少了一個母親。
想想，難道會有那麼美麗的女人，
美到不願你耕耘她處女的童貞？
想想，難道會有那麼美貌的男子，
竟然蠢到自甘墳塋，斷子絕孫？
你是你母親的鏡子，在你身上
她喚回自己陽春四月般的芳齡，
透過你垂暮之年的窗口你將看見
自己的黃金歲月，哪怕你臉上有皺紋。

　　若你雖活著卻無意讓後人稱頌，
　　那就獨身而死吧，人去貌成空。

Sonnet 4

Unthrifty loveliness, why does thou spend
Upon thyself thy beauty's legacy?
Nature's bequest gives nothing, but doth lend,
And being frank, she lends to those are free.
Then, beauteous niggard, why does thou abuse
The bounteous largess given thee to give?
Profitless usurer, why dost thou use
So great a sum of sums yet canst not live?
For having traffic with thyself alone,
Thou of thyself thy sweet self dost deceive,
Then how when Nature calls thee to be gone:
What acceptable audit canst thou leave?
Thy unused beauty must be tombed with thee,
Which used, lives th' executor to be.

4

揮霍成性的人，為什麼你把
美的遺產耗光在你的自身？
造化只出借卻不會饋贈，
她生性慷慨也只出借慷慨之人。
那麼美麗的吝嗇鬼，你為什麼濫用
造化託你轉交的美麗的禮品？
無利可圖的食利者啊，你為什麼
揮霍了重金，卻仍不能安生？
只因你僅僅和自己買賣經營，
你行騙也只騙了你甜蜜的自身。
那麼當造化有一天喚走你的生命，
你怎能把滿意的清單留與世人？

　　何不如風流，讓後代使你遺貌長依舊，
　　不然你那未被垂顧之美只好殉葬荒丘。

Sonnet 5

Those hours that with gentle work did frame
The lovely gaze where every eye doth dwell
Will play the tyrants to the very same,
And that unfair which fairly doth excel;
For never-resting time leads summer on
To hideous winter, and confounds him there,
Sap checked with frost, and lusty leaves quite gone,
Beauty o'er-snowed, and bareness everywhere.
Then were not summer's distillation left
A liquid prisoner pent in walls of glass,
Beauty's effect with beauty were bereft,
Nor it nor no remembrance what it was.
But flowers distilled, though they with winter meet,
Leese but their show; their substance still lives sweet.

5

時光老人曾用精雕細刻

刻出這眾目所歸的美顏,

也會對它施暴虐於某一天,

叫傾國之貌轉眼醜態華現。

因為那周流不息的時光將夏季

帶到可憎的冬季裡摧殘,

令霜凝樹脂,叫茂葉枯卷,

使雪掩美色,呈萬里荒原。

那時若沒有把夏季的香精

提煉成玻璃瓶中的液體囚犯,

美的果實亦將隨美而消殞,

那時美和美的回憶都成過眼雲煙。

　　但如果花經提煉,縱使遇到冬天,

　　雖失掉外表,骨子裡卻仍然清甜。

Sonnet 6

Then let not winter's ragged hand deface
In thee thy summer ere thou be distilled.
Make sweet some vial, treasure thou some place
With beauty's treasure ere it be self-killed.
That use it not forbidden usury,
Which happies those that pay the willing loan:
That's for thyself to breed another thee,
Or ten times happier, be it ten for one;
Ten times thyself were happier than thou art,
If ten of thine ten times refigured thee.
Then what could death do if thou shouldst depart,
Leaving thee living in posterity?
Be not self-willed, for thou art much too fair
To be death's conquest and make worms thine heir.

6

那麼，在你未經提煉之前，
莫讓冬寒粗手把你體內的夏天掠奪，
讓那淨瓶留香吧，快趁你美的精華
未自戕之際，把她們投放進某一個處所，
這樣的投放，並不是非法放債，
它會使借債付息者們打心底裡快活。
這就是說你須得為自己生出另一個人，
倘若能生十個，則會有十倍的快活。
假如你有十個孩子重現你十副肖像，
你現在的幸福就被十倍超過。
這樣一來，你便活在你自己的後代身上，
在你彌留之際，縱是死神也莫奈你何！
　　別太固執了，你是如此絕色無匹，
　　豈能讓死神擄去，讓蛆蟲繼承芳姿。

Sonnet 7

Lo, in the orient when the gracious light
Lifts up his burning head, each under eye
Doth homage to his new-appearing sight,
Serving with looks his sacred majesty,
And having climbed the steep-up heavenly hill,
Resembling strong youth in his middle age,
Yet mortal looks adore his beauty still,
Attending on his golden pilgrimage,
But when from highmost pitch, with weary car,
Like feeble age he reeleth from the day,
The eyes, 'fore duteous, now converted are
From his low tract, and look another way.
So thou, thyself outgoing in thy noon,
Unlooked on diest unless thou get a son.

7

瞧呀,瞧東方仁慈的朝陽抬起了

火紅的頭顱,每一雙塵世的眼睛

都向它初升的景象致敬,

仰望的目光膜拜著神聖的光明。

瞧它登上了陡峭的天峰,

宛如正當盛年的年輕人,

而人間的眼睛依然仰慕他的美貌,

追隨他那金色的旅程。

但當隨倦乏的東輦越過高峰,

他漸漸在遠離白晝,如老邁之人,

於是那從前恭候的目光就不再追逐

他下行之道而轉顧他途。

　　而你呵,也一樣,如今正值赫日當午,

　　若不養個兒子,便會死而無人盼顧。

Shakespeare's Sonnets

Sonnet 8

Music to hear, why hear'st thou music sadly?
Sweets with sweets war not, joy delights in joy.
Why lov'st thou that which thou receiv'st not gladly,
Or else receiv'st with pleasure thine annoy?
If the true concord of well-tuned sounds
By unions married do offend thine ear,
They do but sweetly chide thee, who confounds
In singleness the parts that thou shouldst bear.
Mark how one string, sweet husband to another,
Strikes each in each by mutual ordering,
Resembling sire and child and happy mother,
Who all in one one pleasing note do sing;
Whose speechless song, being many, seeming one,
Sings this to thee: 'Thou single wilt prove none.'

8

你就是音樂卻為何聽著音樂傷情?

美妙和美妙不為敵,樂與樂總同根。

為什麼你愛本不願接受的事物,

或為什麼甘願與憂悶共處一尊?

假如諸聲相配共調出諧曲真情

確實曾經干擾過你的清聽,

這只是甜蜜的責備,你不該孤音自賞,

損害了你應該奏出的和聲。

瞧,這根弦與另一根弦,宛若夫妻,

一根振響,一根相應,弦弦共鳴,

這猶如父親,兒子和快樂之母,

同聲合唱出悅耳的佳音。

　　他們無詞的歌,雖有各種,聽來卻相同。

　　唱的總是你:「若獨身絕種,便萬事皆空。」

Sonnet 9

Is it for fear to wet a widow's eye
That thou consum'st thyself in single life?
Ah, if thou issueless shalt hap to die,
The world will wail thee like a makeless wife.
The world will be thy widow and still weep
That thou no form of thee hast left behind,
When every private widow well may keep
By children's eyes her husband's shape in mind.
Look what an unthrift in the world doth spend
Shifts but his place, for still the world enjoys it;
But beauty's waste hath in the world an end,
And kept unused, the user so destroys it.
No love toward others in that bosom sits
That on himself such murd'rous shame commits.

9

難道是因為懼怕寡婦的淚眼飄零，
你才用獨身生活燒盡你自身？
啊，假如你不幸無後而溘然長逝，
世界將為你慟哭，宛若喪偶的未亡人。
這世界就是你守寡的妻子，她哭啊哭，
哭的是你未留下自己的形影
不像別的寡婦可以靠孩子的眼神
便使丈夫的音容長鎖寸心。
瞧吧，浪子在世雖揮金如土，
也不過錢財易位世人總還有享受的份。
但塵世之美一去將不復再回，
存而不用，終將在美人手裡喪生。
　　既然對自己都會進行可恥的謀殺，
　　這樣的胸腔裡怎容得下對人的愛心。

Sonnet 10

For shame deny that thou bear'st love to any,
Who for thyself art so unprovident.
Grant, if thou wilt, thou art beloved of many,
But that thou none lov'st is most evident;
For thou art so possessed with murd'rous hate
That 'gainst thyself thou stick'st not to conspire,
Seeking that beauteous roof to ruinate
Which to repair should be thy chief desire.
O, change thy thought, that I may change my mind!
Shall hate be fairer lodged than gentle love?
Be as thy presence is gracious and kind,
Or to thyself at least kind-hearted prove.
Make thee another self for love of me,
That beauty still may live in thine or thee.

10

慚愧呀,你就別對人張揚你所謂的愛心,
既然你對自己的將來都缺乏安頓。
姑且承認有許多人對你鍾情
但更明顯的卻是你對誰也不曾傾心。
因為你胸中裝滿的是怨毒與仇恨,
竟不惜陰謀殘害你的自身。
你銳意要摧毀那美麗的秀容,
竟忘了修繕它才是你的本份。
啊,改變你的態度,我也會改變我的,
難道恨比愛反更能在房裡容身?
讓你的內心和外表同樣仁慈吧,
或者至少對你自己發點善心。
  你若是真愛我,就另造一個你,
  好讓美藉你或你的後代永保青春。

Sonnet 11

As fast as thou shalt wane, so fast thou grow'st
In one of thine, from that which thou departest,
And that fresh blood which youngly thou bestow'st
Thou mayst call thine when thou from youth convertest.
Herein lives wisdom, beauty, and increase;
Without this, folly, age, and cold decay.
If all were minded so, the times should cease,
And threescore year would make the world away.
Let those whom nature hath not made for store,
Harsh, featureless, and rude, barrenly perish.
Look whom she best endowed she gave the more,
Which bounteous gift thou shouldst in bounty cherish.
She carved thee for her seal, and meant thereby,
Thou shouldst print more, not let that copy die.

11

迅速地萎縮，一如你迅速地成長──
在你那個之內，那個你進出兩由的地方，
你年輕時貢獻的一注精血若存，
你不再年輕時便成為你收穫的對象，
那其中活躍著智慧、美麗而繁榮昌盛，
而不是愚蠢、衰老和朽敗的冰涼。
若天下都聽獨身主張，則滅宗滅族，
不出六十年，世界也會消亡。
讓造化使無心傳宗接代的人
變得醜陋、粗暴、無後而死亡，
而造化的寵愛者得到最多的恩賜，
這些豐厚的饋贈你都理當珍存。
　　她刻你是要把你作為一枚圓章，
　　多多蓋印，豈可讓圓章徒有虛名！

Sonnet 12

When I do count the clock that tells the time,
And see the brave day sunk in hideous night;
When I behold the violet past prime,
And sable curls, all silvered o'er with white;
When lofty trees I see barren of leaves,
Which erst from heat did canopy the herd,
And summer's green all girded up in sheaves
Borne on the bier with white and bristly beard:
Then of thy beauty do I question make
That thou among the wastes of time must go,
Since sweets and beauties do themselves forsake,
And die as fast as they see others grow;
And nothing 'gainst Time's scythe can make defence
Save breed, to brave him when he takes thee hence.

12

當我細數報時的鐘聲敲響,
眼看可怖夜色吞噬白晝光芒;
當我看到紫羅蘭香消玉殞,
黝黑的捲髮漸漸披上銀霜;
當我看見木葉脫盡的高樹,
曾帳篷般為牧羊人帶來陰涼,
一度青翠的夏苗現在被捆打成束,
載上靈車,連同白色堅脆的麥芒,
於是我不禁為你的美色擔憂,
你也會遲早沒入時間的荒涼,
既然甘美的事物總是會自暴自棄,
眼看後來者居上自己卻快速地消亡,
　　所以沒有什麼能擋住時間的鐮刀,
　　除非你謝世之後留下了兒郎。

Sonnet 13

O that you were yourself! But, love, you are
No longer yours than you yourself here live.
Against this coming end you should prepare,
And your sweet semblance to some other give.
So should that beauty which you hold in lease
Find no determination; then you were
[Yourself] again after yourself's decease,
When your sweet issue your sweet form should bear.
Who lets so fair a house fall to decay,
Which husbandry in honour might uphold
Against the stormy gusts of winter's day,
And barren rage of death's eternal cold?
O, none but unthrifts, dear my love, you know.
You had a father, let your son say so.

13

啊,願你就是你自身,但是愛啊,
你擁有自己的時間長不過你的生命,
勢不可免的末日會來,你該做好準備,
把你那嬌美的形象轉讓與別人,
這樣一來,你那租借來的美色,
就總不會到期——一旦你殞命,
你會再一次成為活生生的自己,
因為你的後嗣會保留你的原形。
誰會讓如此美麗的房舍傾圮,
假如細心的照料會贏來無損,
使它免遭受隆冬的狂風凜冽,
和死神橫掃時的冷酷無情?
　　哦,只有浪子才會這樣,愛,你既知道,
　　你自己有父親,就該讓你兒子也有父親。

Sonnet 14

Not from the stars do I my judgement pluck,
And yet methinks I have astronomy;
But not to tell of good or evil luck,
Of plagues, of dearths, or seasons' quality.
Nor can I fortune to brief minutes tell,
'Pointing to each his thunder, rain, and wind,
Or say with princes if it shall go well
By oft predict that I in heaven find;
But from thine eyes my knowledge I derive,
And, constant stars, in them I read such art
As truth and beauty shall together thrive
If from thyself to store thou wouldst convert.
Or else of thee this I prognosticate:
Thy end is truth's and beauty's doom and date.

14

我不是從星辰得出我的結論,

可我似乎對占星也不學而精,

但我不想要去預知吉凶禍福,

我不要去卜瘟疫,測氣候,占年成。

我不能為分分秒秒算出命運,

說每一刻有什麼雷、雨和風雲。

我也不能憑上蒼暗授的什麼天機,

披露帝王將相是走紅還是背運。

我只是從你的雙眼這一對恆星

破謎解惑推導出下述學問:

假如你回心轉意哺育兒孫,

真和美就永遠繁榮共存。

　　要不然我就會這樣給你算命:

　　你的死期也就是真與美的墓門。

Sonnet 15

When I consider every thing that grows
Holds in perfection but a little moment,
That this huge stage presenteth naught but shows
Whereon the stars in secret influence comment;
When I perceive that men as plants increase,
Cheered and checked even by the self-same sky;
Vaunt in their youthful sap, at height decrease,
And wear their brave state out of memory:
Then the conceit of this inconstant stay
Sets you most rich in youth before my sight,
Where wasteful Time debateth with decay
To change your day of youth to sullied night;
And all in war with time for love of you,
As he takes from you, I engraft you new.

15

當我忖思,一切充滿生機的事物
都只能興旺短暫的時光,
在世界這大舞臺上呈現的一切
都暗中受制於天上的星象;
當我看到人類像草木一樣滋長,
任同一個蒼天隨意褒貶抑揚,
少壯時神采飛動,盛極而漸衰,
往日的鼎盛貌逐步被人遺忘。
正是這種對無常世界的憂思,
使我想到你充滿青春朝氣的形象,
而今肆虐的時間和朽腐為伍,
要化你青春的潔白為黑夜的骯髒。
　　為了與你相愛,我將向時間提出宣戰,
　　它使你枯萎,我令你移花接木換新裝。

Sonnet 16

But wherefore do not you a mightier way
Make war upon this bloody tyrant, Time,
And fortify yourself in your decay
With means more blessed than my barren rhyme?
Now stand you on the top of happy hours,
And many maiden gardens yet unset,
With virtuous wish would bear your living flowers,
Much liker than your painted counterfeit.
So should the lines of life that life repair
Which this time's pencil or my pupil pen
Neither in inward worth nor outward fair
Can make you live yourself in eyes of men.
To give away yourself keeps yourself still,
And you must live drawn by your own sweet skill.

16

但為什麼你不用更有效的方法
去反抗這嗜血的時間魔王,
或用更幸福的手段來抵抗衰朽,
卻反借重我這不育的詩行?
如今你置身於桃花運的頂峰之上,
有許多處女園等待你栽插紅芳,
殷切地盼望著你植下活花朵朵,
花兒比你的畫像更顯出你的真相。
所以生命只能靠生命線維繫,
不論是我的塗鴉還是當代的畫匠
都不能使你活現在人們的心房,
讓你內在和外在的美色昭彰。
　　放棄你自己將反使你自己長在,
　　想生存就得靠把傳宗妙技發揚。

Sonnet 17

Who will believe my verse in time to come
If it were filled with your most high deserts?
Though yet, heaven knows, it is but as a tomb
Which hides your life, and shows not half your parts.
If I could write the beauty of your eyes
And in fresh numbers number all your graces,
The age to come would say 'This poet lies;
So should my papers, yellowed with their age,
Be scorned, like old men of less truth than tongue,
And your true rights be termed a poet's rage
And stretched metre of an antique song.
But were some child of yours alive that time,
You should live twice: in it, and in my rhyme.

17

將來誰會相信我這些歌唱,
如果你至高的美德溢滿詩章?
儘管天知道這只是一座墳墓,
葬著你的命,難使你德行張揚。
如果我能描摹你流盼的美目,
把你的千嬌百媚織入我的詩行,
未來的時代會說:「這位詩人撒謊——
這樣的天工之筆從未描過塵世的面龐。」
於是我的詩稿帶著歲月的熏黃,
將受到嘲弄,像嘲弄饒舌的老頭一樣。
你應得的禮讚被看作是詩人的狂想,
或看作一首古曲的虛飾誇張:
  但如果那時候你有子孫健在,
  你就雙倍活於他身和我的詩行。

Sonnet 18

Shall I compare thee to a summer's day?
Thou art more lovely and more temperate.
Rough winds do shake the darling buds of May,
And summer's lease hath all too short a date.
Sometime too hot the eye of heaven shines,
And often is his gold complexion dimmed,
And every fair from fair sometime declines,
By chance or nature's changing course untrimmed;
But thy eternal summer shall not fade
Nor lose possession of that fair thou ow'st,
Nor shall death brag thou wander'st in his shade
When in eternal lines to time thou grow'st.
So long as men can breathe or eyes can see,
So long lives this, and this gives life to thee.

18

或許我可用夏日將你作比方,
但你比夏日更可愛也更溫良。
夏風狂作常會摧落五月的嬌蕊,
夏季的期限也未免還不太長。
有時候天眼如炬人間酷熱難當,
但轉瞬又金面如晦常惹雲遮霧障。
每一種美都終究會凋殘零落,
或見棄於機緣,或受挫於天道無常。
然而你永恆的夏季卻不會終止,
你優美的形象也永遠不會消亡,
死神難誇口說你在他的羅網中遊蕩,
只因你借我的詩行便可長壽無疆。
　　只要人口能呼吸,人眼看得清,
　　我這詩就長存,使你萬世留芳。

Sonnet 19

Devouring Time, blunt thou the lion's paws,
And make the earth devour her own sweet brood;
Pluck the keen teeth from the fierce tiger's jaws,
And burn the long-lived phoenix in her blood.
Make glad and sorry seasons as thou fleet'st,
And do whate'er thou wilt, swift-footed Time.
To the wide world and all her fading sweets.
But I forbid thee one most heinous crime:
O, carve not with thy hours my love's fair brow,
Nor draw no lines there with thine antique pen.
Him in thy course untainted do allow
For beauty's pattern to succeeding men.
Yet do thy worst, old Time; despite thy wrong
My love shall in my verse ever live young.

19

吞噬一切的流光,你磨鈍了獅爪,
使大地把自己的幼嬰吞掉,
你從猛虎的嘴中撬出了利牙,
教長壽的鳳凰被活活燃燒。
你行蹤過處,令季節非哭即笑,
呵,捷足的時間,你為所欲為吧,
踏遍河山萬里,摧殘盡百媚千嬌。
但,住手!有一樁罪,罪大不容饒:
你休在我愛人的美額上擅逞刻刀,
你休用古舊的畫筆在上面亂抹線條!
你且容他任流光飛逝不改原貌。
但把美的楷模偏留與後世人瞧。
　　時光老頭啊,憑你展淫威、施強暴,
　　有我詩卷,我愛人便韶華常駐永不凋。

Sonnet 20

A woman's face with Nature's own hand painted
Hast thou, the master-mistress of my passion;
A woman's gentle heart, but not acquainted
With shifting change as is false women's fashion;
An eye more bright than theirs, less false in rolling,
Gilding the object whereupon it gazeth;
A man in hue, all hues in his controlling,
Which steals men's eyes and women's souls amazeth.
And for a woman wert thou first created,
Till Nature as she wrought thee fell a-doting,
And by addition me of thee defeated
By adding one thing to my purpose nothing.
But since she pricked thee out for women's pleasure,
Mine be thy love and thy love's use their treasure.

20

你，我詩中的情婦兼情郎，
是造化親自繪出你女性的面龐，
你雖有女人的柔婉的心，但沒有
輕佻女人慣有的反覆無常。
你的眼比她們的更真誠更明亮，
目光流盼處，事物頓染上金黃。
你有男子的風采，令一切風采低頭，
使眾男子神迷，使眾女人魂飛魄蕩。
造化的本意是要讓你做一個女人，
但在造你時卻如喝了迷魂湯，
胡亂安一個東西在你身上，我於是
不能承歡於你，那東西我派不上用場。
　　既然造化造你是供女人取樂，
　　給我愛，但給女人做愛的寶藏。

Sonnet 21

So is it not with me as with that Muse
Stirred by a painted beauty to his verse,
Who heaven itself for ornament doth use,
And every fair with his fair doth rehearse,
Making a couplement of proud compare
With sun and moon, with earth, and sea's rich gems,
With April's first-born flowers, and all things rare
That heaven's air in this huge rondure hems.
O let me, true in love, but truly write,
And then believe me my love is as fair
As any mother's child, though not so bright
As those gold candles fixed in heaven's air.
Let them say more that like of hearsay well;
I will not praise that purpose not to sell.

21

我並不像那一位詩人一樣,
因畫布上的美人便感而成章,
連蒼天都成為他筆底的裝飾,
驅群美以襯托他那美貌之郎,
滿紙繡詞麗句、比附誇張,
海底、珠寶、大地、月亮和太陽,
四月的鮮花,以及一切奇珍異物,
環掛長空,直面宇宙的浩茫。
啊,讓我忠實地愛、忠實地寫吧,
請相信我,我的愛雖難與
蒼穹金燭台般的星斗爭光,
但其美恰如任何母親的孩子一樣。

  讓別的詩人說盡陳詞濫調吧,
  我不是販夫,絕不自賣又自誇。

Sonnet 22

My glass shall not persuade me I am old
So long as youth and thou are of one date;
But when in thee time's furrows I behold,
Then look I death my days should expiate.
For all that beauty that doth cover thee
Is but the seemly raiment of my heart,
Which in thy breast doth live, as thine in me;
How can I then be elder than thou art?
O therefore, love, be of thyself so wary
As I, not for myself, but for thee will,
Bearing thy heart, which I will keep so chary
As tender nurse her babe from faring ill.
Presume not on thy heart when mine is slain:
Thou gav'st me thine not to give back again.

22

鏡子無法使我相信你已衰老，
只要你和青春還是同道，
但當我看見你臉上的皺紋，
我就料想自己的死期已到。
因為你全身上下的美麗外表，
不過是我內心的真實寫照，
你胸中的紅心也在我心中燃燒，
我豈能膽敢比你早露衰兆？
哦，我的愛，你一定要保重自身，
正如我為你而非為我把自己照料，
擁著你的心，我自會謹慎萬分，
像乳娘護嬰，生怕他染上病苗。

　　如果我的心已先碎，你的又豈能自保，
　　你既已把心給了我，我豈能原物回交。

Sonnet 23

As an unperfect actor on the stage
Who with his fear is put besides his part,
Or some fierce thing replete with too much rage
Whose strength's abundance weakens his own heart,
So I, for fear of trust, forget to say
The perfect ceremony of love's rite,
And in mine own love's strength seem to decay,
O'ercharged with burden of mine own love's might.
O, let my books be then the eloquence
And dumb presagers of my speaking breast,
Who plead for love, and look for recompense
More than that tongue that more hath more expressed.
O, learn to read what silent love hath writ;
To hear with eyes belongs to love's fine wit.

23

像一個演戲的新手初次登場，
慌亂裡把臺詞忘個精光，
又像是猛獸胸懷滿腔怒火，
雄威太盛反令怯心惶惶。
我也因缺乏自信而忘掉
愛情儀式全部的適當辭章，
我的愛力似乎在變得枯弱，
是愛的神威壓彎了我的脊樑。
啊，請讓我的詩卷雄辯滔滔，
無聲地吐出我滿蓄情懷的訴狀，
它為我的愛申辯，且尋求賠償，
遠勝過那喋喋不休的巧舌如簧。
　　哦，請用眼聽愛的智慧發出的清響，
　　請學會去解讀沉默之愛寫下的詩章。

Shakespeare's Sonnets

Sonnet 24

Mine eye hath played the painter, and hath steeled
Thy beauty's form in table of my heart.
My body is the frame wherein 'tis held,
And perspective it is best painter's art;
For through the painter must you see his skill
To find where your true image pictured lies,
Which in my bosom's shop is hanging still,
That hath his windows glazed with thine eyes.
Now see what good turns eyes for eyes have done:
Mine eyes have drawn thy shape, and thine for me
Are windows to my breast, wherethrough the sun
Delights to peep, to gaze therein on thee.
Yet eyes this cunning want to grace their art:
They draw but what they see, know not the heart.

24

我的眼睛是畫家,將你
美的形象畫在我的心版上,
我的軀體是畫框,向框裡透視,
你會發現傳神筆觸來自高超的畫匠,
你需要通過畫師去把他的妙技觀摩,
去尋找你真容的畫像在何處隱藏,
那畫像永遠掛在我胸內的畫店裡,
你明亮的雙眼是那畫店的玻璃窗,
瞧眼睛和眼睛互相幫了多大的忙,
我的眼畫下你的形象,你的眼睛
則作我胸室的明窗,太陽也樂於
穿過那窗櫺去偷看、去凝視你,
 然而我的眼睛還缺乏更高的才能:
 能畫目之所見,卻難畫心之所藏。

Sonnet 25

Let those who are in favour with their stars
Of public honour and proud titles boast,
Whilst I, whom fortune of such triumph bars,
Unlooked for joy in that I honour most.
Great princes' favourites their fair leaves spread
But as the marigold at the sun's eye,
And in themselves their pride lies buried,
For at a frown they in their glory die.
The painful warrior famoused for fight,
After a thousand victories once foiled
Is from the book of honour razed quite,
And all the rest forgot for which he toiled.
Then happy I, that love and am beloved
Where I may not remove nor be removed.

25

且讓那些鴻運亨通的人們,
誇耀其高位與顯赫的虛名,
我雖無緣側身幸運者之堂,
卻意外使深心的追求如願以償。
得寵的王臣雖能春風得意於一時,
但如金盞花隨日出日落乍開還閉,
一旦龍顏震怒,他們便香消玉殞,
昔日的榮華威風轉眼化作煙塵。
含辛茹苦、名播沙場的將士,
千百次征戰所向披靡,一朝敗績,
姓名便立刻從功勞簿上消逝,
從前的赫赫戰功再無人提起:

　　而我,多幸福,既被人愛又能愛人,
　　我堅定,別人也休想動搖我一分。

Sonnet 26

Lord of my love, to whom in vassalage
Thy merit hath my duty strongly knit,
To thee I send this written embassage
To witness duty, not to show my wit;
Duty so great which wit so poor as mine
May make seem bare in wanting words to show it,
But that I hope some good conceit of thine
In thy soul's thought, all naked, will bestow it,
Till whatsoever star that guides my moving
Points on me graciously with fair aspect,
And puts apparel on my tottered loving
To show me worthy of thy sweet respect.
Then may I dare to boast how I do love thee;
Till then, not show my head where thou mayst prove me.

26

愛呵,您是我的主,您的德行
早已贏得我臣服於您的忠心,
我而今繕寫謹呈上片紙詩行,
只為鞠躬盡職,不敢小露鋒芒。
重命在肩,可憐我才疏學陋,
赤膽忠心找不到詩句遮羞。
盼只盼您靈魂深處的奇思妙想
使我粗裸的才具有個安息之邦。
等到某一顆星星導引著我前進,
為我施恩般照亮美境濃蔭,
使我這襤褸之愛罩上錦套頭,
方配得上您仁慈浩蕩的皇恩。
　　惟有那時我才敢誇口對您柔情似水,
　　我從前躲閃,是怕您考驗我的雄威。

Sonnet 27

Weary with toil I haste me to my bed,
The dear repose for limbs with travel tired;
But then begins a journey in my head
To work my mind when body's work's expired;
For then my thoughts, from far where I abide,
Intend a zealous pilgrimage to thee,
And keep my drooping eyelids open wide,
Looking on darkness which the blind do see:
Save that my soul's imaginary sight
Presents thy shadow to my sightless view,
Which like a jewel hung in ghastly night
Makes black night beauteous and her old face new,
Lo, thus by day my limbs, by night my mind,
For thee, and for myself, no quiet find.

27

心倦神疲,我急欲上床休息,
好安頓旅途倦乏的肢體。
然而軀體的遠足勞作剛停,
心靈上卻開始了新的長征。
我雖遠處他鄉,但我的思想
卻朝聖般奔赴您的身旁。
我強睜大睡意矇矓的雙眼,
把盲人也看得見的黑暗凝望。
我借助靈魂的想像的目光
已窺見您在黑暗中的形象,
宛如恐怖之夜高懸的明珠,
令蒼老的黑夜新生,一片輝煌。
　　瞧吧,我白晝的身子,黑夜的心,
　　為您,為我,全都無法安寧。

Sonnet 28

How can I then return in happy plight,
That am debarred the benefit of rest,
When day's oppression is not eased by night,
But day by night and night by day oppressed,
And each, though enemies to either's reign,
Do in consent shake hands to torture me,
The one by toil, the other to complain
How far I toil, still farther off from thee?
I tell the day to please him thou art bright,
And do'st him grace when clouds do blot the heaven;
So flatter I the swart-complexioned night
When sparkling stars twire not thou gild'st the even.
But day doth daily draw my sorrows longer,
And night doth nightly make grief's strength seem stronger.

28

既然我白天黑夜不能安心獨處,
白晝的壓迫在夜晚得不到消除,
日以繼夜,夜以繼日,愁煩更苦,
我又怎能夠使快樂的心境恢復?
日和夜雖然原本互相為敵,
但折磨我時卻聯手作戰配合默契。
一個讓我辛勞,一個讓我哀怨
說我跋涉得遠,卻離你更遠。
我討好白晝,告訴它你四射光芒,
縱雲遮麗日,你可使白晝輝煌。
我又這樣去巴結陰暗的夜晚,
說一旦星星消殘,你可使夜空光亮。
　　然而白天卻一天天使我憂心加重
　　夜晚則一晚晚使我愁思更濃。

Sonnet 29

When, in disgrace with Fortune and men's eyes,
I all alone beweep my outcast state,
And trouble deaf heaven with my bootless cries,
And look upon myself and curse my fate,
Wishing me like to one more rich in hope,
Featured like him, like him with friends possessed,
Desiring this man's art and that man's scope,
With what I most enjoy contented least:
Yet in these thoughts myself almost despising,
Haply I think on thee, and then my state,
Like to the lark at break of day arising
From sullen earth, sings hymns at heaven's gate;
For thy sweet love remembered such wealth brings
That then I scorn to change my state with kings.

29

面對命運的拋棄,世人的冷眼,
我唯有獨自把飄零的身世悲歎。
我曾徒然地呼喚聾耳的蒼天,
詛咒自己的時運,顧影自憐。
我但願,願胸懷千般心願,
願有三朋六友和美貌之顏;
願有才華蓋世,有文采斐然,
唯對自己的長處,偏偏看輕看淡。
我正耽於這種妄自菲薄的思想,
猛然間想到了你,頓時景換情遷,
我忽如破曉的雲雀凌空振羽,
謳歌直上天門,把蒼茫大地俯瞰。
　　但記住你柔情招來財無限,
　　縱帝王屈尊就我,不與換江山。

Sonnet 30

When to the sessions of sweet silent thought
I summon up remembrance of things past,
I sigh the lack of many a thing I sought,
And with old woes new wail my dear time's waste.
Then can I drown an eye unused to flow
For precious friends hid in death's dateless night,
And weep afresh love's long since cancelled woe,
And moan th' expense of many a vanished sight.
Then can I grieve at grievances foregone,
And heavily form woe to woe tell o'er
The sad account of fore-bemoaned moan,
Which I new pay as if not paid before.
But if the while I think on thee, dear friend,
All losses are restored, and sorrows end.

30

我有時醉心於沉思默想，
把過往的事物細細品嘗；
我慨歎許多未曾如願之事，
舊恨新愁使我痛悼蹉跎的時光。
不輕彈的熱淚擠滿我的雙眼，
我慟哭親朋長眠於永夜的孤魂，
歎多少故人舊物如逝水難追，
勾起我傷懷久已訣別的風情。
憂心再起為的是流年遺恨，
舊緒重翻件件令我愁鎖心庭。
有多少傷心事如舊債難數，
今日重了帳，彷彿當時未還清。
　　但只要此刻我想到了你，朋友，
　　損失全挽回，愁雲恨霧頓時收！

Sonnet 31

Thy bosom is endeared with all hearts
Which I by lacking have supposed dead,
And there reigns love, and all love's loving parts,
And all those friends which I thought buried.
How many a holy and obsequious tear
Hath dear religious love stol'n from mine eye
As interest of the dead, which now appear
But things removed that hidden in thee lie!
Thou art the grave where buried love doth live,
Hung with the trophies of my lovers gone,
Who all their parts of me to thee did give:
That due of many now is thine alone.
Their images I loved I view in thee,
And thou, all they, hast all the all of me.

31

你胸懷珍貴,因為你胸藏一切心上人,
我和他們無緣,曾以為他們全都喪生。
在你那胸腔裡,愛及愛的一切可愛的品行,
都和我曾以為葬身其內的朋友共處一尊。
對死者熱烈、虔誠的眷戀曾偷走
我聖潔、哀傷的淚兒如湧泉奔流,
而今回首,才明白這些過世的幽魂
不過是移居另處,安住在你的胸襟。
你庇護著我埋葬了的愛,你是孤墳,
墳內滿掛著我那些過世戀人的戰利品,
他們把我的一片癡心都轉贈給你消受,
於是許多人共有的愛而今你獨自佔有。
 在你的身上我看見我那些情人的形象,
 你是他們全體,我的一切都是你的收藏。

Sonnet 32

If thou survive my well-contented day
When that churl Death my bones with dust shall cover,
And shalt by fortune once more resurvey
These poor rude lines of rhy deceased lover,
Compare them with the bett'ring of the time,
And though they be outstripped by every pen,
Reserve them for my love, not for their rhyme
Exceeded by the height of happier men.
O then vouchsafe me but this loving thought:
'Had my friend's Muse grown with this growing age,
A dearer birth than this his love had brought
To march in ranks of better equipage;
But since he died, and poets better prove,
Theirs for their style I'll read, his for his love.'

32

如果你的壽限長過我坦然面對的天命之數,
當無情的死神掩埋我的屍骨於一坯黃土,
而你偶然翻讀你這位死去的情郎
曾在世時寫下的粗鄙、拙劣的詩章,
你讓它們與時下的傑構佳篇相比,
發現它們遜色於每一位詩人的手筆,
論技巧總不如哪些幸運兒的碩果輝煌,
但請保留我的吧,只為愛不為韻腳的鏗鏘。
呵,但願你開懷大度儘量把我往好處想:
假如我朋友的天賦能與世推移,
憑他的真愛必能吟出更好的詩行,
使他能與當世高手並駕齊驅。
　　而他既已不幸辭世,詩人們也詩藝倍增,
　　我欣賞後者的文采,但品讀前者的愛心。

Sonnet 33

Full many a glorious morning have I seen
Flatter the mountain tops with sovereign eye,
Kissing with golden face the meadows green,
Gilding pale streams with heavenly alchemy;
Anon permit the basest clouds to ride
With ugly rack on his celestial face,
And from the forlorn world his visage hide,
Stealing unseen to west with this disgrace.
Even so my sun one early morn did shine
With all triumphant splendour on my brow;
But out, alack, he was but one hour mine;
The region cloud hath masked him from me now.
Yet him for this my love no whit disdaineth:
Suns of the world may stain when heaven's sun staineth.

33

多少個明媚輝煌的清晨,我看見

威嚴的朝陽把四射光芒灑滿山巔,

它那金色的臉兒貼緊碧綠的草原,

用上界的煉金術使慘澹的溪水璀璨。

然而倏忽間,忍對片片烏雲,

黑沉沉橫過它那莊嚴的面影,

使遺棄的下界難睹其尊容,

它於是蒙羞戴恥暗沉下碧霄九重。

我的太陽也曾如此四射光芒,

在一個清晨輝煌於我的前額之上。

可是唉!我只能一時承受其恩寵,

須臾雲遮霧障,再不復重睹它的金容。

　　然而我對他的愛心並不稍稍有減,

　　天上的太陽會暗,人世的更理所當然。

Sonnet 34

Why didst thou promise such a beauteous day
And make me travel forth without my cloak,
To let base clouds o'ertake me in my way,
Hiding thy brav'ry in their rotten smoke?
'Tis not enough that through the cloud thou break
To dry the rain on my storm-beaten face,
For no man well of such a salve can speak
That heals the wound and cures not the disgrace.
Nor can thy shame give physic to my grief;
Though thou repent, yet I have still the loss.
Th' offender's sorrow lends but weak relief
To him that bears the strong offence's cross.
Ah, but those tears are pearl which thy love sheds,
And they are rich, and ransom all ill deeds.

34

為什麼你期許如此的晴空麗日，
使我輕裝上路，不慮遮風避雨，
而一旦我涉足中途，你卻讓濃雲翻飛，
使你四射的光芒在迷霧中消失？
縱然你後來又穿破密雲濃霧，
曬乾我臉上暴風疾雨留下的珠痕，
然而無人會稱讚你這種治病藥膏：
醫得了創傷，卻醫不了心靈的痛楚。
你的羞慚雖冰釋我徹骨的憂愁，
你雖痛悔再三，我卻惆悵依舊。
犯罪者引咎自責，又怎能夠驅除
替人受過者內心的極度悲苦！
　　但是，唉，你流出的情淚是顆顆明珠，
　　價值連城，使你的一切罪惡獲得救贖。

Sonnet 35

No more be grieved at that which thou hast done:
Roses have thorns, and silver fountains mud.
Clouds and eclipses stain both moon and sun,
And loathsome canker lives in sweetest bud.
All men make faults, and even I in this,
Authorizing thy trespass with compare,
Myself corrupting salving thy amiss,
Excusing thy sins more than thy sins are;
For to thy sensual fault I bring in sense
Thy adverse party is thy advocate
And 'gainst myself a lawful plea commence.
Such civil war is in my love and hate
That I an accessory needs must be
To that sweet thief which sourly robs from me.

35

毋須再為你的所作所為悲傷：
玫瑰有刺，明泉也難免濁水泥浪，
烏雲和日蝕月蝕會讓日月無光，
可惡的蚊蟲會在嬌蕾裡躲藏。
人人有過失，我也一樣：
為文過飾非，不惜濫打比方，
自我貶損為的是開脫你的罪狀，
你過失萬千，我絕不將你問罪公堂。
對於你的浪蕩之行我詳加體諒──
我這作原告的反為你辯護伸張──
我提起訴訟，告的卻是我自己，
我的愛和恨就這樣掀起一場內仗。
　　到頭來，我落得淪為你的幫兇，
　　幫你這甜偷兒無情打劫自己的心房。

Sonnet 36

Let me confess that we two must be twain
Although our undivided loves are one;
So shall those blots that do with me remain
Without thy help by me be borne alone.
In our two loves there is but one respect,
Though in our lives a separable spite
Which, though it alter not love's sole effect,
Yet doth it steal sweet hours from love's delight.
I may not evermore acknowledge thee
Lest my bewailed guilt should do thee shame,
Nor thou with public kindness honour me
Unless thou take that honour from thy name.
But do not so. I love thee in such sort
As thou being mine, mine is thy good report.

36

儘管我們的愛天衣無縫、渾然一體,
我卻得承認我們畢竟在肉體上分離。
這樣一來,我身上不光彩的疤痕,
不勞你分憂,我自當獨自擔承。
是我們之間的摯愛把我們合二為一,
儘管在現實裡我們有兩個身軀。
兩個身軀也改不了我們愛的專一、真純,
但畢竟會耗費掉些許甜蜜的光陰。
我從此或不再張揚你是我的知己,
以防我可悲的過失玷污你的英名;
你也不要當眾賦予我殊榮,
除非你甘冒名聲受損的厄運。
可是別,別把我的話兒當真,
　　須知我的愛是這樣一種愛:
　　你既屬於我,我的好名聲你也有份。

Sonnet 37

As a decrepit father takes delight
To see his active child do deeds of youth,
So I, made lame by Fortune's dearest spite,
Take all my comfort of thy worth and truth;
For whether beauty, birth, or wealth, or wit,
Or any of these all, or all, or more,
Entitled in thy parts do crowned sit,
I make my love engrafted to this store.
So then I am not lame, poor, nor despised,
Whilst that this shadow doth such substance give
That I in thy abundance am sufficed
And by a part of all thy glory live.
Look what is best, that best I wish in thee;
This wish I have, then ten times happy me.

37

正像陽精萎頓的父親喜歡觀看
年輕氣盛的孩子演示風流韻事,
我雖曾蒙受命運最大的摧殘,
卻也能從你的美德與真誠獲得快意。
美色、門第、才華或財富
無論其中一樣或更多或全部,
都在你身上發揮得恰到好處,
我於是把自己的愛植入你這寶庫。
從此,我不再殘廢,或受人鄙視。
既然這庇護之所讓充實代替了幻影,
我當滿足於你的富裕豐盈,
活下去,憑藉你這一抹濃蔭。
　　我但望你的庫內有無價的奇珍至寶,
　　而一旦如願,我便十倍地快樂逍遙。

Sonnet 38

How can my Muse want subject to invent
While thou dost breathe, that pour'st into my verse
Thine own sweet argument, too excellent
For every vulgar paper to rehearse?
O, give thyself the thanks if aught in me
Worthy perusal stand against thy sight;
For who's so dumb that cannot write to thee,
When thou thyself dost give invention light?
Be thou the tenth Muse, ten times more in worth
Than those old nine which rhymers invocate,
And he that calls on thee, let him bring forth
Eternal numbers to outlive long date.
If my slight Muse do please these curious days,
The pain be mine, but thine shall be the praise.

38

我的詩神豈會缺乏詩材與詩思，
只要你活著，你自己就是甜美的主題。
你湧動於我的詩章，如此美妙，
要描摹你，焉能謬託蹩腳詩人的頹筆？
假如我的詩有聊供垂鑒之處，
那也全是由於你的惠顧。
正是你點燃了想像的火把，
才令無動於衷者為你詩情勃發。
你超過你前面的九位老繆斯十倍，
你將名列十位詩神榜而無愧。
且讓求助你的詩人詩花怒放，
寫出超越永恆的不朽篇章。
　　倘這苛求時代容得下我微薄的詩才，
　　我當萬苦不辭只寫詩將你謳歌膜拜。

Sonnet 39

O, how thy worth with manners may I sing
When thou art all the better part of me?
What can mine own praise to mine own self bring,
And what is't but mine own when I praise thee?
Even for this let us divided live,
And our dear love lose name of single one,
That by this separation I may give
That due to thee which thou deserv'st alone.
O absence, what a torment wouldst thou prove
Were it not thy sour leisure gave sweet leave
To entertain the time with thoughts of love,
Which time and thoughts so sweetly doth deceive,
And that thou teachest how to make one twain
By praising him here who doth hence remain!

39

假如你和我本來就共為一體,
我又怎能只歌頌你且歌頌得宜?
我自己歌頌自己有什麼意味?
我若歌頌你不也等於自吹自擂?
正因為如此,我們應該分離獨處,
使我們的愛各有區別開來的名義。
借助於這種區別,我才可以獻出
你理應獨得的那一份頌詞。
然而,別離呵,若非借你單調的餘暇,
以愛思來消磨時光使之甜蜜有加,
若非你使愛哄騙了時光與思想,
若非你教我如何化單為雙,

  使我藉機在此將遠方的人兒歌吟,
  呵,別離,你又將何等令我傷魂!

Sonnet 40

Take all my loves, my love, yea, take them all:
What hast thou then more than thou hadst before?
No love, my love, that thou mayst true love call
All mine was thine before thou hadst this more.
Then if for my love thou my love receivest,
I cannot blame thee for my love thou usest;
But yet be blamed if thou this self deceivest
By wilful taste of what thyself refusest.
I do forgive thy robb'ry, gentle thief,
Although thou steal thee all my poverty;
And yet love knows it is a greater grief
To bear love's wrong than hate's known injury.
Lascivious grace, in whom all ill well shows,
Kill me with spites, yet we must not be foes.

40

把我的所愛者奪走吧,全都奪走,
且看你是否比從前多添了朋儕?
愛呵,你找不到別的什麼愛可稱為真愛,
我所愛者原是你的,即便此前你未曾到手。
那麼,假如你為愛我而奪走我的愛,
我豈能責怪你為愛我而將我的愛消受。
但假如你自己騙自己,執意要嘗,
你不願接受的東西,我就真想罵你個夠。
姑且原諒你的竊行,你這來頭不小的小偷,
儘管你把我的全部家當統統擄走。
然而愛是明白的:忍受愛的屈從俯就
要比忍受恨的公開傷害更令人憂愁。
    可人的風流啊,連你的惡行都成了美德,
    咬殺我吧,但我們絕不成為冤家對頭。

Sonnet 41

Those pretty wrongs that liberty commits
When I am sometime absent from thy heart
Thy beauty and thy years full well befits,
For still temptation follows where thou art.
Gentle thou art, and therefore to be won;
Beauteous thou art, therefore to be assailed;
And when a woman woos, what woman's son
Will sourly leave her till he have prevailed?
Ay me, but yet thou mightst my seat forbear,
And chide thy beauty and thy straying youth
Who lead thee in their riot even there
Where thou art forced to break a two fold truth:
Hers by thy beauty tempting her to thee,
Thine by thy beauty being false to me.

41

你趁我不在你心頭的時候,
便放蕩不羈,肆意風流。
論青春論美色你二者兼備,
行跡所至,總會有誘惑追求。
你文雅高貴,當然有人想贏得你芳心;
你美色出眾,必有人尾隨你大獻殷勤。
面對一個女人的勾引,哪一個男子
會忍心拒絕不乘機享受桃花運?
但是唉,求你別把我的位兒占,
求你管住你的美色和浪蕩的青春。
求你別隨心所欲去闖下亂子,
到頭來被迫毀掉雙重的信譽:
  毀她和我的,因你用美色使她失身;
  毀你和我的,因你的美色對我不忠實。

Sonnet 42

That thou hast her, it is not all my grief,
And yet it may be said I loved her dearly;
That she hath thee is of my wailing chief,
A loss in love that touches me more nearly.
Loving offenders, thus I will excuse ye:
Thou dost love her because thou know'st I love her,
And for my sake even so doth she abuse me,
Suff'ring my friend for my sake to approve her.
If I lose thee, my loss is my love's gain,
And losing her, my friend hath found that loss:
Both find each other, and I lose both twain,
And both for my sake lay on me this cross.
But here's the joy: my friend and I are one.
Sweet flattery! Then she loves but me alone.

42

你佔有了她,我並不因此過度傷情,
雖說我對她也還算有一片癡心。
她佔有了你,這才令我嚎啕欲絕,
這至愛的喪失使我幾乎痛徹心庭。
情場作案者呵我只好這樣來為你們開脫:
你愛她,不過是因為我是她的情人;
她騙我,也因為她對我無限傾心,
所以才讓我的朋友與她試享雲雨情。
我雖失掉你,我情人卻因之有所補,
我雖失掉她,我朋友卻因之有所進。
你倆互進互補,我卻兩頭落空。
只是為我著想,你們才讓我嘗盡酸辛。

　　我且把單相思當苦中樂:你我本同根,
　　隨她如何愛,愛的也只可能是我本人。

Sonnet 43

When most I wink, then do mine eyes best see,
For all the day they view things unrespected;
But when I sleep, in dreams they look on thee,
And, darkly bright, are bright in dark directed.
Then thou, whose shadow shadows doth make bright,
How would thy shadow's form form happy show
To the clear day with thy much clearer light,
When to unseeing eyes thy shade shines so!
How would, I say, mine eyes be blessed made
By looking on thee in the living day,
When in dead night thy fair imperfect shade
Through heavy sleep on sightless eyes doth stay!
All days are nights to see till I see thee,
And nights bright days when dreams do show thee me.

43

我的眼睛閉得緊緊,卻反能看得清清

他們白日裡所見之物,多半是淡淡平平。

但當我的雙眼在夢中向你凝望,

它們如暗夜焰火頓時四照光明。

你眼中觀照的形象既能使黑暗發出光芒,

它們又怎會在大白天裡用更強的光亮

形成令人銷魂的場景,

我雖閉起了雙眼,你的形象卻如此鮮明。

那麼,唉,我的雙眼要怎樣才會交上好運,

以便在青天白日裡也能目睹你的倩影,

不然我就只能在死夜於沉沉的酣睡中,

用緊閉的雙眸觀摩你飄忽的芳容。

　　看不到君顏,每一個白日都如黑暗陰晦,

　　夜夜成了白天,因為只在夜夢裡我們才相會。

Sonnet 44

If the dull substance of my flesh were thought,
Injurious distance should not stop my way;
For then, despite of space, I would be brought
From limits far remote where thou dost stay.
No matter then although my foot did stand
Upon the farthest earth removed from thee;
For nimble thought can jump both sea and land
As soon as think the place where he would be.
But ah, thought kills me that I am not thought,
To leap large lengths of miles when thou art gone,
But that, so much of earth and water wrought,
I must attend time's leisure with my moan,
Receiving nought by elements so slow
But heavy tears, badges of either's woe.

44

假如我這笨重的肉體如輕靈的思想,
那麼山重水複也擋不住我振翅翱翔,
我將視天涯海角如咫尺之隔,
不遠鴻途萬里,孤飛到你身旁。
此刻我的雙足所立的處所
雖與你遠隔千山又有何妨,
只要一想到你棲身的地方,
這電疾般的思想便會穿洲過洋。
然而可嘆我並非空靈的思緒
能騰躍追隨你的行蹤越嶺跨江,
我只是泥和水鑄成的凡胎肉體,
惟有用浩嘆伺奉蹉跎的時光。

  唉,無論土和水於我都毫無補益,
  它們只標誌著哀愁令我淚飛如雨。

Sonnet 45

The other two, slight air and purging fire,
Are both with thee wherever I abide;
The first my thought, the other my desire,
These present-absent with swift motion slide;
For when these quicker elements are gone
In tender embassy of love to thee,
My life, being made of four, with two alone
Sinks down to death, oppressed with melancholy,
Until life's composition be recurred
By those swift messengers returned from thee,
Who even but now come back again assured
Of thy fair health, recounting it to me.
This told, I joy; but then no longer glad,
I send them back again and straight grow sad.

45

還有兩種元素,淨火與輕風,
不論我棲身何處總伴隨你的行蹤。
風是我的思想,火是我的欲望,
它們神出鬼沒,來去何匆匆。
這兩個輕快的元素一旦它往,
去為我向你傳達愛的心衷,
我的生命便奄奄待斃愁心難整,
不堪其中一對,因為它本由元素構成。
我的生命的結構要想復原,
除非這兩個輕靈的使者回還,
呵,它們現在就回來了,提到
你的健康狀況切切傳語報平安。
　　我聞信不由大喜,可嘆喜而不久,
　　再次送走它們後,我仍濃愁依舊。

Sonnet 46

Mine eye and heart are at a mortal war
How to divide the conquest of thy sight.
Mine eye my heart thy picture's sight would bar,
My heart, mine eye the freedom of that right.
My heart doth plead that thou in him dost lie,
A closet never pierced with crystal eyes;
But the defendant doth that plea deny,
And says in him thy fair appearance lies.
To 'cide this title is impanelled
A quest of thoughts, all tenants to the heart,
And by their verdict is determined
The clear eye's moiety and the dear heart's part,
As thus: mine eye's due is thy outward part,
And my heart's right thy inward love of heart.

46

我的眼睛和心兒正吵做一團，
爭搶著要分享你的芳顏，
眼睛不許心兒親睹你的倩影，
心兒不許眼睛把你自由觀看。
心兒聲稱你本來就棲居在它的領土，
無人能窺其堂奧即便有雪亮的眼珠，
然而眼睛全不認心的申訴，
堅持說惟有明眸使你花容長駐。
這一場公案究竟如何定，
起伏心潮終竟得斷案有主。
左思右想才定出個判詞兒，
使亮眼不污，柔心不負：

> 你外表的美由我的眼睛佔有，
> 你內在的愛由我的心兒消受。

Sonnet 47

Betwixt mine eye and heart a league is took,
And each doth good turns now unto the other.
When that mine eye is famished for a look,
Or heart in love with sighs himself doth smother,
With my love's picture then my eye doth feast,
And to the painted banquet bids my heart.
Another time mine eye is my heart's guest
And in his thoughts of love doth share a part.
So either by thy picture or my love,
Thyself away art present still with me;
For thou not farther than my thoughts canst move,
And I am still with them, and they with thee;
Or if they sleep, thy picture in my sight
Awakes my heart to heart's and eye's delight.

47

我的眼睛和心達成了協議,
相約同舟共濟互助互利。
當眼睛無法將尊容親睹,
或當癡戀的心兒為嘆息所苦,
眼兒便呈現戀人的肖像,
且邀心兒共享這畫宴的盛況。
有時眼睛也應邀赴心兒的宴席,
共流連忘返於銷魂的情思。
這一來借了你的肖像或我的愛戚,
遠離的你卻仍與我廝守相隨。
隨你浪跡天涯也擺不脫我的苦思,
我緊跟著它,它緊纏著你。
　　縱然情思入夢,你的肖像在我的眼裡,
　　也會喚醒寸心,叫心兒眼兒皆大歡喜。

Sonnet 48

How careful was I when I took my way
Each trifle under truest bars to thrust,
That to my use it might unused stay
From hands of falsehood, in sure wards of trust.
But thou, to whom my jewels trifles are,
Most worthy comfort, now my greatest grief,
Thou best of dearest and mine only care
Art left the prey of every vulgar thief.
Thee have I not locked up in any chest
Save where thou art not, though I feel thou art
Within the gentle closure of my breast,
From whence at pleasure thou mayst come and part;
And even thence thou wilt be stol'n, I fear,
For truth proves thievish for a prize so dear.

48

啓程之時我是多麼謹慎小心,
把一切日用物件全上鎖封存,
堅壁固房務使竊賊望而縮手,
他日取用之時當使塵封如舊。
然而你令我的珠寶無光,
昨日使我至樂,今宵叫我斷腸,
你是我的肺和肝、我惟一的心頭肉,
而今卻無遮無攔任鼠竊狗偷。
我無法把你鎖進金箱銀箱,
只鎖你在我溫柔的胸膛,
我感到你似在非在,似有非有,
因為這地方你原可以來去自由。
 怕的是隱祕如此你仍會被偷被搶,
 對這樣的寶物縱海誓山盟也廢紙一張。

Sonnet 49

Against that time – if ever that time come
When I shall see thee frown on my defects,
Whenas thy love hath cast his utmost sum,
Called to that audit by advised respects;
Against that time when thou shalt strangely pass
And scarcely greet me with that sun, thine eye,
When love converted from the thing it was
Shall reasons find of settled gravity:
Against that time do I ensconce me here
Within the knowledge of mine own desert,
And this my hand against myself uprear
To guard the lawful reasons on thy part.
To leave poor me thou hast the strength of laws,
Since why to love I can allege no cause.

49

怕的是那個時候,那時候一旦到來,
你會皺起雙眉嫌我是個障礙,
那時候你已燒盡愛的每一滴燈油,
你深思熟慮後說:讓我們現在分手——
怕的是那個時候,那時候你漠然走來,
不再用你太陽般的眼睛射出歡迎的光彩,
那時候愛已冰冷,翻臉再不認人,
行為粗暴乖張,理由卻總是充分——
怕的是那個時候我這才惟求自保,
把自己的長短得失掂量個分曉,
為你我舉手宣誓,反對我自己,
站在你的立場上捍衛你的權益——
　　要想拋棄我你有的是法律依據,
　　而我自己對這一場愛卻講不出道理。

Sonnet 50

How heavy do I journey on the way,
When what I seek – my weary travel's end
Doth teach that ease and that repose to say
'Thus far the miles are measured from thy friend.'
The beast that bears me, tired with my woe,
Plods dully on to bear that weight in me,
As if by some instinct the wretch did know
His rider loved not speed, being made from thee.
The bloody spur cannot provoke him on
That sometimes anger thrusts into his hide,
Which heavily he answers with a groan
More sharp to me than spurring to his side;
For that same groan doth put this in my mind:
My grief lies onward and my joy behind.

50

這一場跋涉真令人神疲力倦,
你如願以償地走到困頓旅途的終點,
一陣安逸接一場酣夢忽叫我省悟:
我和你又分隔得多麼遙遠。
壓在我身下的坐騎不堪我的苦痛,
緩緩前行,承載著我那一團沈重。
可憐的馬兒似由某一種本能得知,
騎手愛的不是速度,越快越遠離開你。
帶血的馬刺也激不起牠前進的興頭,
發怒的騎手於是猛刺進牠的皮肉。
馬兒忽然沈重地回報出一聲呻吟,
我聽了鑽心更甚於馬刺刺進牠的身。

　　正是這一聲低吟叫我突然清醒──
　　快樂已成身後事,惆悵眼前生。

Sonnet 51

Thus can my love excuse the slow offence
Of my dull bearer when from thee I speed:
From where thou art why should I haste me thence?
Till I return, of posting is no need.
O, what excuse will my poor beast then find
When swift extremity can seem but slow?
Then should I spur, though mounted on the wind;
In winged speed no motion shall I know.
Then can no horse with my desire keep pace;
Therefore desire, of perfect'st love being made,
Shall neigh no dull flesh in his fiery race;
But love, for love, thus shall excuse my jade:
Since from thee going he went wilful-slow,
Towards thee I'll run and give him leave to go.

51

我既然是離你他往,

又何須要行色倉皇;

不是回頭路,更何須馬不收韁。

愛呵,我的坐騎的魯鈍原不是大罪,

除非是歸程,縱電疾如火也不算匆忙。

可憐的馬兒啊,那時才罪重當誅,

我當快馬加鞭,電掣般乘風飛揚——

雖展翅凌空亦不覺其迅,那時節,

沒一匹馬兒可與我如熾的欲火爭強。

呵,這集愛之大成的欲望絕非一團死肉,

自當引頸長嘯於火焰般的飛揚。

然而一報還一報,原諒我這玉驄的魯鈍吧——

　　既然牠抽身離你時有意磨磨蹭蹭,

　　我要正面向你,讓牠由著性兒狂奔。

Shakespeare's Sonnets

Sonnet 52

So am I as the rich whose blessed key
Can bring him to his sweet up-locked treasure,
The which he will not ev'ry hour survey,
For blunting the fine point of seldom pleasure.
Therefore are feasts so solemn and so rare
Since seldom coming, in the long year set
Like stones of worth they thinly placed are,
Or captain jewels in the carcanet.
So is the time that keeps you as my chest,
Or as the wardrobe which the robe doth hide,
To make some special instant special blest
By new unfolding his imprisoned pride.
Blessed are you whose worthiness gives scope,
Being had, to triumph; being lacked, to hope.

52

我像是富翁，懷藏能交好運的鑰匙，
可隨時啟開那緊鎖深院的密室。
我不願每時每刻造訪那幽居，
只怕磨鈍難得的快感的鋒鏑。
喜慶佳節之所以莊嚴、珍貴，
因為一年裡難得有幾次發生，
就好比是項鍊上的珍珠寶貝，
雖疏疏落落，卻更光彩照人。
同樣珍貴的是那一段時光，
我看顧它如寶庫衣櫥，時時留心，
猛然間展示出囚禁起來的瑰寶，
頓使那難逢的一刻格外引人銷魂。
　　好一個走運的你，有如此神通無限，
　　有你時，其樂無比，無你時望眼欲穿。

Sonnet 53

What is your substance, whereof are you made,
That millions of strange shadows on you tend?
Since every one hath, every one, one shade,
And you, but one, can every shadow lend.
Describe Adonis, and the counterfeit
Is poorly imitated after you.
On Helen's cheek all art of beauty set,
And you in Grecian tires are painted new.
Speak of the spring and foison of the year:
The one doth shadow of your beauty show,
The other as your bounty doth appear;
And you in every blessed shape we know.
In all external grace you have some part,
But you like none, none you, for constant heart.

53

你的本質是什麼？由什麼材料構成，
為何有千萬個他者之影侍奉在你身邊？
既然每一個人只可能有一個形象，
為什麼你一人卻能夠出借影子萬千？
為阿董尼寫生吧，而他的肖像，
不過是你原型的拙劣模仿。
縱使在海倫的頰上濫施盡美容絕技，
描出的肖像也只是穿上希臘古裝的你。
即使用春媚秋豐作個比方，
前者只是你本色的投影，
後者只是你豐饒的表象，
世間萬種美色都無非是你的變形。
　　大千世界的嫵媚無不與你相通，
　　說起忠誠守節，卻無人與你相同。

Shakespeare's Sonnets

Sonnet 54

O how much more doth beauty beauteous seem
By that sweet ornament which truth doth give!
The rose looks fair, but fairer we it deem
For that sweet odour which doth in it live.
The canker-blooms have full as deep a dye
As the perfumed tincture of the roses,
Hang on such thorns, and play as wantonly
When summer's breath their masked buds discloses;
But for their virtue only is their show
They live unwooed and unrespected fade,
Die to themselves. Sweet roses do not so;
Of their sweet deaths are sweetest odours made:
And so of you, beauteous and lovely youth,
When that shall vade, by verse distils your truth.

54

假如有真所賦予的甜蜜作裝潢,
美就一定會更加美色無雙!
嬌美的玫瑰之所以會使人感到它更美,
是因為它那甜美的活色生香。
野薔薇花枝招展但卻沒有香味,
憑色相卻可與馥郁的玫瑰爭輝,
當夏風撩開了它們隱蔽的花蕾,
它們綻放枝頭,自覺千嬌百媚。
但它們的德行只是其外表,
開時無人羨其色,謝時無人嘆其凋,
只落得悄然自殞,豈如玫瑰濃馨揚,
雖紅顏薄命,骨煉也成餘香。
　　你也一樣,美麗可愛的「少年人」,
　　當色去香空,我的詩會提煉出你的純精。

Shakespeare's Sonnets

Sonnet 55

Not marble nor the gilded monuments
Of princes shall outlive this powerful rhyme,
But you shall shine more bright in these contents
Than unswept stone besmeared with sluttish time.
When wasteful war shall statues overturn,
And broils root out the work of masonry,
Nor Mars his sword nor war's quick fire shall burn
The living record of your memory.
'Gainst death and all oblivious enmity
Shall you pace forth; your praise shall still find room
Even in the eyes of all posterity
That wear this world out to the ending doom.
So, till the judgment that yourself arise,
You live in this, and dwell in lovers' eyes.

55

王公大族的雲石豐碑或鍍金牌坊

終將朽敗,惟我強勁的詩章萬壽無疆。

我的詩行將使你大放光彩,

遠勝過塵封的石頭,暗淡的時光。

毀滅性的戰爭將推翻石像,

暴亂亦將會掃蕩盡鐵壁銅牆。

然而你如果長留在這活的記錄裡,

任利劍兵火毀不掉你的遺芳。

你高視闊步面對死亡和彌天之恨,

縱然千秋萬代之後世人的雙眼,

都還會讀到我這記錄對你的頌揚,

哪怕那時候人類的末日已來到世上。

  所以,直到最後的審判你站起來之際,

  你將住在戀人的眼裡,活於我不朽的詩行。

Sonnet 56

Sweet love, renew thy force, be it not said
Thy edge should blunter be than appetite,
Which but today by feeding is allayed,
Tomorrow sharpened in his former might.
So, love, be thou; although today thou fill
Thy hungry eyes even till they wink with fullness,
Tomorrow see again, and do not kill
The spirit of love with a perpetual dullness.
Let this sad int'rim like the ocean be
Which parts the shore where two contracted new
Come daily to the banks, that when they see
Return of love, more blest may be the view;
Or call it winter, which, being full of care,
Makes summer's welcome, thrice more wished, more rare.

56

寶貝兒愛呵,快重振你的雄風,
別讓人說你的欲念超過你行動的刀鋒。
前日如願以償,飽餐一頓,
明日舊情復發,餓像更兇。
愛呵,你也一樣,今日你那餓眼
飽食後欲開還閉,睡眼惺忪,
明日重新勃啓之後,絕不能
萎靡不振,阻塞了情精愛洪。
讓這淒艷的暫歇如同大海,
隔開兩片陸地,有情人日日岸邊逢,
一旦看到有愛浪歸來滔滔滾滾,
其情其景或更令之情深意濃。
　　或讓這間隔像冬天般鬱悶,無精打采,
　　好使盛夏的來臨更令人三倍地喜愛。

Sonnet 57

Being your slave, what should I do but tend
Upon the hours and times of your desire?
I have no precious time at all to spend,
Nor services to do, till you require;
Nor dare I chide the world-without-end hour
Whilst I, my sovereign, watch the clock for you,
Nor think the bitterness of absence sour
When you have bid your servant once adieu.
Nor dare I question with my jealous thought
Where you may be, or your affairs suppose,
But like a sad slave stay and think of nought
Save where you are how happy you make those.
So true a fool is love that in you will,
Though you do anything, he thinks no ill.

57

既是你的奴僕,我只能聊盡愚忠
滿足你的慾望,一刻也不放鬆。
我雖無寶貴的時間供自己驅遣,
卻可聽命於你帳下,垂首鞠躬。
我不敢抱怨大千世界綿邈無窮,
我只為你,我的君王,看守時鐘。
你吩咐我這個僕從悄然退下,
我不敢多想,離思別緒愁更濃。
我不敢心懷嫉妒,暗自猜疑,
你幹什麼勾當,何處留下行蹤。
我只如一個憂戚的奴僕,頭腦空空,
只玄想你身形到處多少人為你怦然心動。
　　唉,我這植入你慾田的愛真是蠢豬,
　　眼見你為所欲為,卻淡然視若無睹。

Sonnet 58

That god forbid, that made me first your slave,
I should in thought control your times of pleasure,
Or at your hand th' account of hours to crave,
Being your vassal bound to stay your leisure.
O, let me suffer, being at your beck,
Th' imprisoned absence of your liberty,
And patience, tame to sufferance, bide each check,
Without accusing you of injury.
Be where you list, your charter is so strong
That you yourself may privilege your time
To what you will; to you it doth belong
Yourself to pardon of self-doing crime.
I am to wait, though waiting so be hell,
Not blame your pleasure, be it ill or well.

58

使我臣服於你之前的神靈

不准我限制你行樂的光陰,

不准我弄清你如何度過每一個時辰。

既是你的臣下,只能任你縱情。

啊,就讓我遵命自囚於孤獨的牢獄吧,

你既然肆意逍遙,二意三心。

讓我默然忍受你的聲聲呵斥,

絕不對你的傷害抱有微詞。

你隨意而往吧,既然你享有特權。

可自由支配你的時間,

為所欲為吧,你已有特權,

可將你的一切罪行赦免。

  我絕不責你尋歡作樂,管他是惡是善,

  我只能牢囚般期待,哪怕把牢底坐穿。

Sonnet 59

If there be nothing new, but that which is
Hath been before, how are our brains beguiled,
Which, labouring for invention, bear amiss
The second burden of a former child!
O that record could with a backward look
Even of five hundred courses of the sun
Show me your image in some antique book
Since mind at first in character was done,
That I might see what the old world could say
To this composed wonder of your frame;
Whether we are mended or whe'er better they,
Or whether revolution be the same
O, sure I am the wits of former days
To subjects worse have given admiring praise.

59

假如天下無新東西，萬古如斯，
哪麼我們的大腦多麼容易癡迷，
儘管想發明創造用心良苦，
到頭來免不了是依樣畫葫蘆。①
啊，但願有歷史記載供我追溯，
至少五百年前的某一本古書，
你的形象早已顯現在哪裡，
自從人的思想開始用文字來記錄，
我想看看古人曾用什麼妙筆，
描摹過你光彩照人的絕世風姿，
究竟是我們技高還是他們筆拙，
究竟千古輪迴是否毫無新意。
　　但有一事我敢肯定，前朝的才子，
　　曾濫用筆墨讚美過遠不如你的主題。

---

①原文是：無非是生出一個已經有過的嬰孩。

Sonnet 60

Like as the waves make towards the pebbled shore,
So do our minutes hasten to their end,
Each changing place with that which goes before;
In sequent toil all forwards do contend.
Nativity, once in the main of light,
Crawls to maturity, wherewith being crowned
Crooked eclipses 'gainst his glory fight,
And Time that gave doth now his gift confound.
Time doth transfix the flourish set on youth,
And delves the parallels in beauty's brow;
Feeds on the rarities of nature's truth,
And nothing stands but for his scythe to mow.
And yet to times in hope my verse shall stand,
Praising thy worth despite his cruel hand.

60

宛如不息滔滔長波拍岸,

我們的分分秒秒匆匆奔赴向前。

後浪推前浪,今天接明天,

奮發趨行,你爭我趕。

那初生於光海中的生命,

漸次成熟,直達輝煌的頂端,

便有兇惡的日蝕與之爭光鬥彩,

時間於是將自己的餽贈搗個稀爛。

韶華似刀會割掉青春的面紗,

會在美人的前額上刻下溝槽,

會吞掉自然天成的奇珍異寶,

唉,天下萬物沒一樣躲得過它的鐮刀。

  但我的詩章將逃過時間的毒手,

  謳歌你的美德,越千年而不朽。

Sonnet 61

Is it thy will thy image should keep open
My heavy eyelids to the weary night?
Dost thou desire my slumbers should be broken
While shadows like to thee do mock my sight?
Is it thy spirit that thou send'st from thee
So far from home into my deeds to pry,
To find out shames and idle hours in me,
The scope and tenor of thy jealousy?
O no; thy love, though much, is not so great.
It is my love that keeps mine eye awake,
Mine own true love that doth my rest defeat,
To play the watchman ever for thy sake.
For thee watch I whilst thou dost wake elsewhere,
From me far off, with others all too near.

61

你是否執意要用你的倩影似幻,

使我於漫漫長夜強睜睡眼?

你是否想讓我夜不成眠,

用你的幻影把我的視覺欺騙?

你是否已經派遣你的魂兒

離家別舍只為把我的行動偵探?

你是想證實你的嫉妒和猜疑,

察明我是如何放浪荒誕?

啊,不,你的愛雖多卻尚未如此深厚,

這原是我自己的愛使我久久不合眼,

我的真愛使我不能休息,

為你的緣故總高昂著睜眼的臉——

　　我為你守夜,你卻在某地背著我,

　　徹夜不眠地跟別的人耳鬢廝磨。

Sonnet 62

Sin of self-love possesseth all mine eye,
And all my soul, and all my every part;
And for this sin there is no remedy,
It is so grounded inward in my heart.
Methinks no face so gracious is as mine,
No shape so true, no truth of such account,
And for myself mine own worth do define
As I all other in all worths surmount.
But when my glass shows me myself indeed,
Beated and chapped with tanned antiquity,
Mine own self-love quite contrary I read;
Self so self-loving were iniquity.
'Tis thee, myself that for myself I praise,
Painting my age with beauty of thy days.

62

我的眼、靈魂和全身每一部份，
全都充斥著自戀的罪行，
沒有藥物能治癒這種邪惡，
因為它的病根深繫在我心的底層。
我自忖自己的魅力或不可限量，
論體態、論赤誠我都蓋世無雙。
如果需要對自己的長處做一個估計，
我自認方方面面都會技壓群芳。
然而攬鏡自照方見出自己的真顏，
只可憐衰鬢橫紋、滿面色蒼蒼。
而今我終於看透自家自戀病，
自我溺愛無異是罪惡纏身。
　　為你也為我自己把你稱讚，
　　好用你的青春之美點綴我的衰年。

Sonnet 63

Against my love shall be as I am now,
With Time's injurious hand crushed and o'erworn;
When hours have drained his blood and filled his brow
With lines and wrinkles; when his youthful morn
Hath travell'd on to age's steepy night,
And all those beauties whereof now he's king
Are vanishing, or vanished out of sight,
Stealing away the treasure of his spring:
For such a time do I now fortify
Against confounding age's cruel knife,
That he shall never cut from memory
My sweet love's beauty, though my lover's life.
His beauty shall in these black lines be seen,
And they shall live, and he in them still green.

63

有一天我的美人會沈淪如我,
被時間的毒手搗碎、折磨,
歲月會吸乾其血液並在他額上
罩上一層皺紋,他的青春的朝陽,
將掠過中天峭壁似暮年之夜,
他所曾佔有的一切風流美色,
當不翼而飛,化為烏有,
他那春情勃發的活力去也悠悠——
為抵抗這樣的時候,我把戰壕深築,
誓擋住殘年流月的霜刀利斧,
它們縱能奪去我愛人的生命,
卻無法不讓其風韻百代如初。

　　他的美將長留於這些墨染的詩行,
　　行行詩不老,詩裡人自萬古流芳。

Sonnet 64

When I have seen by Time's fell hand defaced
The rich proud cost of outworn buried age;
When sometime lofty towers I see down razed,
And brass eternal slave to mortal rage;
When I have seen the hungry ocean gain
Advantage on the kingdom of the shore,
And the firm soil win of the wat'ry main,
Increasing store with loss and loss with store;
When I have seen such interchange of state,
Or state itself confounded to decay,
Ruin hath taught me thus to ruminate:
That Time will come and take my love away.
This thought is as a death, which cannot choose
But weep to have that which it fears to lose.

64

曾見過時間的毒手跋扈飛揚，

抹掉前代留下的豪華與榮光；

曾見過高樓俄傾成平地，

浩劫塵封了鐵壁銅牆。

曾見過饑海層翻滾滾浪，

吞蝕了周遭沃土岸邊王；

轉眼陸地又反攻侵大海，

唉，這念頭令我死一般迷茫，

得失盈虧無常事，幾度滄桑，

睜淚眼強抓住惟恐失掉的情郎，

看透了天道循環無止歇，

今日偉大風光，難免他日淒涼。

　　天災人禍，忍教我細細思量，

　　時辰若到，我的愛終究水淹蒼江。

Sonnet 65

Since brass, nor stone, nor earth, nor boundless sea,
But sad mortality o'ersways their power,
How with this rage shall beauty hold a plea,
Whose action is no stronger than a flower?
O how shall summer's honey breath hold out
Against the wreckful siege of battering days
When rocks impregnable are not so stout,
Nor gates of steel so strong, but Time decays?
O fearful meditation! Where, alack,
Shall Time's best jewel from Time's chest lie hid,
Or what strong hand can hold his swift foot back,
Or who his spoil of beauty can forbid?
O none, unless this miracle have might:
That in black ink my love may still shine bright.

65

既然大地滄海巨石堅金
均難與無常永世並存，
那麼，嬌若柔花的美
又如何能與死的嚴威抗衡？
夏日的嫩蕊香風如何能擋住
來日霜刀雪劍的摧凌？
縱然是壁立巉岩鋼門如鑄，
終必在時間的磨礪下消殞。
啊，令人膽寒的思想！我只能哀歎，
時間的珍珠難免埋進時間的荒墳。
問，可有巨手能擋住這過客般的光陰？
可有猛士能止住他掠奪美物的暴行？
　　沒有，沒有，要使我的愛輝耀千載，
　　惟一的高招是借我的墨跡顯聖通靈。

Sonnet 66

Tired with all these, for restful death I cry:
As to behold desert a beggar born,
And needy nothing trimmed in jollity,
And purest faith unhappily forsworn,
And gilded honour shamefully misplaced,
And maiden virtue rudely strumpeted,
And right perfection wrongfully disgraced,
And strength by limping sway disabled,
And art made tongue-tied by authority,
And folly, doctor-like, controlling skill,
And simple truth miscalled simplicity,
And captive good attending captain ill.
Tired with all these, from these would I be gone,
Save that to die, I leave my love alone.

66

難耐不平事,何如悄然去泉台:

休說是天才,偏生作乞丐,

人道是草包,偏把金銀戴,

說什麼信與義,眼見無人睬,

道什麼榮與辱,全是瞎安排,

少女童貞可憐遭橫暴,

堂堂正義無端受掩埋,

跛腿權勢反弄殘了擂臺漢,

墨客騷人宮府門前口難開,

蠢驢們偏掛著指謎釋惑教授招牌,

多少真話錯喚作愚魯癡呆,

善惡易位,小人反受大人拜。

　　不平,難耐,索不如一死化纖埃,

　　待去也,又怎好讓愛人獨守空階?

Sonnet 67

Ah, wherefore with infection should he live
And with his presence grace impiety,
That sin by him advantage should achieve
And lace itself with his society?
Why should false painting imitate his cheek,
And steal dead seeming of his living hue?
Why should poor beauty indirectly seek
Roses of shadow, since his rose is true?
Why should he live, now Nature bankrupt is,
Beggared of blood to blush through lively veins,
For she hath no exchequer now but his,
And proud of many, lives upon his gains?
O, him she stores to show what wealth she had
In days long since, before these last so bad.

67

唉,為什麼他會棲身濁世,
其風采令朽腐亦假作神奇,
靠他的蔭庇罪惡亦討得便宜,
和他套近乎美稱為近朱者赤。
為什麼騙人的畫師取像於他的真容,
從他那豐神俊采裡只偷去僵死的形式?
既然他的玫瑰才是真玫瑰,為什麼
可憐的美人卻繞道追尋玫瑰的影子?
造化天趣已喪,再無活血在血管中奔流,
為什麼他還要苟安於世?
因為她①只能從他獲得美泉如注,
雖曾有風情萬種,現在都惟他可依。
　　她珍藏了他的以證明許久許久以前,
　　她並非如此匱乏,而是富麗無比。

---

①原文為「她」,各家注文均以為「她」即指造化,權從。
　　　　　　　　　　　　　　　　——譯者

Sonnet 68

Thus is his cheek the map of days outworn,
When beauty lived and died as flowers do now,
Before these bastard signs of fair were born,
Or durst inhabit on a living brow;
Before the golden tresses of the dead,
The right of sepulchres, were shorn away
To live a second life on second head;
Ere beauty's dead fleece made another gay.
In him those holy antique hours are seen
Without all ornament, itself and true,
Making no summer of another's green,
Robbing no old to dress his beauty new;
And him as for a map doth Nature store,
To show false Art what beauty was of yore.

68

他的臉儼然如往古歲月的留紋，

那時的美恰如今日之花自滅自生。

那時虛矯粉飾之美尚未出世，

更不敢在活人的額上兀自存身。

那時死者的金髮尚能安然

長存於墓穴，尚未遭禍於快剪，①

以便在第二個額頭上苟延年命，

好使美艷在別人頭上借髮重生。

在他們身上活現出遠古聖潔的光彩，

天然去雕飾，惟有樸質天真，

不藉他人之綠舖陳夏色，

不掠舊美使華服如新。

　　天教他權作一幅美色活標本，

　　好使假匠人得識古代美人真身。

---

① 莎士比亞時代的製造假髮者常買死人頭髮來加工成新髮。

Sonnet 69

Those parts of thee that the world's eye doth view
Want nothing that the thought of hearts can mend.
All tongues, the voice of souls, give thee that due,
Utt'ring bare truth even so as foes commend.
[Thy] outward thus with outward praise is crowned,
But those same tongues that give thee so thine own
In other accents do this praise confound
By seeing farther than the eye hath shown.
They look into the beauty of thy mind,
And that in guess they measure by thy deeds.
Then, churls, their thoughts — although their eyes were kind
To thy fair flower add the rank smell of weeds.
But why thy odour matcheth not thy show,
The [soil] is this: that thou dost common grow.

69

你那天生麗質可面對眾目睽睽,
真個是你想有多美就有多美。
千嘴萬舌從心底裡為你證明,
這赤裸裸的真理連敵手也難於否認。
你的外表便如此贏得一片頌聲,
但同樣的口舌雖曾為你歌吟,
卻也以變調唱出相反的頌詞,
比起眼睛它們似乎看得更遠更深。
他們仔細探究你內心的美,
猜度揣測憑的是你的行為,
他們和善的目光中,卻有偏狹的思想,
硬將野草味替代你鮮花的奇香。
然而你的花色與花香為何不相配?
因為你不擇地勢隨處綻放花蕾。

Sonnet 70

That thou are blamed shall not be thy defect,
For slander's mark was ever yet the fair.
The ornament of beauty is suspect,
A crow that flies in heaven's sweetest air.
So thou be good, slander doth but approve
[Thy] worth the greater, being wooed of time;
For canker vice the sweetest buds doth love,
And thou present'st a pure unstained prime.
Thou hast passed by the ambush of young days
Either not assailed, or victor being charged;
Yet this thy praise cannot be so thy praise
To tie up envy, evermore enlarged.
If some suspect of ill masked not thy show,
Then thou alone kingdoms of hearts shouldst owe.

70

罵你責你並不是你的過失，

因為美人從來難逃流言蜚語。

世人的猜忌無異是美人的裝飾，

恰如孤鴉飛鳴點綴碧空如洗。

才高德廣，則讒言只能證明

你該領受更大的尊重，世不你欺。

毒蟲惡蛆最偏愛嬌花嫩蕊，

當心呀，你正當妙齡，純潔無疵。

你已越過青春路上的潛敵，

或安然脫險，或得勝班師，

然而對你這樣的讚美還遠遠不夠

為你堵住日益擴大的嫉妒之口。

  倘若惡意的猜忌遮掩不住你的真相，

  那你獨自一人將擁有多少心靈之邦。

Sonnet 71

No longer mourn for me when I am dead
Than you shall hear the surly sullen bell
Give warning to the world that I am fled
From this vile world with vilest worms to dwell.
Nay, if you read this line, remember not
The hand that writ it; for I love you so
That I in your sweet thoughts would be forgot
If thinking on me then should make you woe.
O, if, I say, you look upon this verse
When I perhaps compounded am with clay,
Do not so much as my poor name rehearse,
But let your love even with my life decay,
Lest the wise world should look into your moan
And mock you with me after I am gone.

71

有一天你會聽到陰鬱的鐘聲
向世人宣告我已逃離這污穢的世界
伴隨最齷齪的蛆蟲往另一世界安身,
我勸你千萬不要為我而悲鳴。
還有,你讀這詩行的時候千萬別記掛
這寫詩的手,因為我愛你至深,
惟願被忘卻在你甜甜的思緒裡,
我怕你想到我時會牽動愁心。
哦,我說,如果你垂顧這詩句時,
我或許已化作土石泥塵,
請不要重提我這可憐的名字,
只要你的愛與我的命同葬荒墳。
　　這樣就不怕聰明人看透你的哀怨,
　　在我死後用我作把柄拿你尋開心。

Sonnet 72

O, lest the world should task you to recite
What merit lived in me that you should love,
After my death, dear love, forget me quite;
For you in me can nothing worthy prove
Unless you would devise some virtuous lie
To do more for me than mine own desert,
And hang more praise upon deceased I
Than niggard truth would willingly impart.
O, lest your true love may seem false in this,
That you for love speak well of me untrue,
My name be buried where my body is,
And live no more to shame nor me nor you;
For I am shamed by that which I bring forth,
And so should you, to love things nothing worth.

72

哦，為了防止世人對你究底盤根，
我既身已歿，尚有何德何能
敢蒙你垂青？呵，愛啊，忘掉我，
因為你確實找不到我可愛的鐵證。
除非你能羅織出無害的謊言，
對我大肆吹噓，施朱著粉，
為九泉之下的我捧出更多的頌詞，
全不顧誇張的話當以事實為本，
哦，怕你的真愛又因此顯得虛偽，
怕人說你為了愛對我阿諛奉承。
我倒願我的姓名和肢體同臥荒丘，
免得它苟行於世令你抱慚蒙羞。
　　我因此愧對自己的塗鴉之作，
　　你愛了不值得愛的也會臉紅如火。

Sonnet 73

That time of year thou mayst in me behold
When yellow leaves, or none, or few, do hang
Upon those boughs which shake against the cold,
Bare ruined choirs where late the sweet birds sang.
In me thou seest the twilight of such day
As after sunset fadeth in the west,
Which by and by black night doth take away,
Death's second self, that seals up all in rest.
In me thou seest the glowing of such fire
That on the ashes of his youth doth lie
As the death-bed whereon it must expire,
Consumed with that which it was nourished by.
This thou perceiv'st, which makes thy love more strong,
To love that well which thou must leave ere long.

73

你在我身上會看到這樣的時候,

那時零落的黃葉會殘掛枝頭,

三兩片在寒風中索索發抖,

荒涼的歌壇上不再有甜蜜的歌喉。

你在我身上會看到黃昏時候

落霞消殘,漸沉入西方的天際,

夜幕迅速將它們通通帶走,

恰如死神的替身將一切鎖進牢囚。

你在我身上會看到這樣的火焰,

它在青春的灰燼上閃爍搖頭,

如安臥於臨終之榻,待與

供養火種的燃料一同燒盡燒透。

  看到了這一切,你的愛會更加堅貞,

  愛我吧,我在世的日子已不會太久。

Sonnet 74

But be contented when that fell arrest
Without all bail shall carry me away.
My life hath in this line some interest,
Which for memorial still with thee shall stay.
When thou reviewest this, thou dost review
The very part was consecrate to thee.
The earth can have but earth, which is his due;
My spirit is thine, the better part of me.
So then thou hast but lost the dregs of life,
The prey of worms, my body being dead,
The coward conquest of a wretch's knife,
Too base of thee to be remembered.
The worth of that is that which it contains,
And that is this, and this with thee remains.

74

有一天,當地獄的陰差自地獄來臨
不由分說將我拘走,但不必擔心,
我的詩行與我的生命如藕斷絲連,
宛若紀念舊情之物長隨在你身。
一旦你重讀這些詩行,你會看到
我專為奉獻於你的那一部分,
恰如土本屬於土,理所當然,
那是我的精粹,是我的精神。
因而,我的肉體一旦泯滅,
你失去的不過是生命的渣滓,
是蛆蟲之食和惡棍刀下的懦夫,
太卑賤了,真不配你口誦心記。
　　我這微軀所值全賴有內在之魂,
　　　忠魂化詩句,長伴你度過餘生。

Sonnet 75

So are you to my thoughts as food to life,
Or as sweet-seasoned showers are to the ground;
And for the peace of you I hold such strife
As 'twixt a miser and his wealth is found;
Now proud as an enjoyer, and anon
Doubting the filching age will steal his treasure;
Now counting best to be with you alone,
Then bettered that the world may see my pleasure;
Sometime all full with feasting on your sight,
And by and by clean starved for a look;
Possessing or pursuing no delight
Save what is had or must from you be took.
Thus do I pine and surfeit day by day,
Or gluttoning on all, or all away.

75

如同生命需要食糧，你哺育著我的思想，
好比春天的酥雨為大地注滿瓊漿。
我珍愛你給我的安寧，心中又苦痛驚惶，
好比懷揣金玉的守財奴時時怕偷一樣。
他一會兒財大而氣粗，志得而意滿，
一會兒又怕這慣盜時代偷走他的寶藏。
才覺得人間至樂是與你單獨相處，
忽而又希望世人均知我得志情場。
有時飽眼餐秀色飽得如享盛宴。
有時餓眼看情人餓得心裡發慌。
天下有諸多快樂我不佔也不求，
只獨守已得之樂，只盼望你的獎賞。
  我就這樣每日饑飽、欠缺又豐隆，
  要麼饕餮大嚼，要麼腹內空空。

Sonnet 76

Why is my verse to barren of new pride,
So far from variation or quick change?
Why, with the time, do I not glance aside
To new-found methods and to compounds strange?
Why write I still all one, ever the same,
And keep invention in a noted weed,
That every word doth almost tell my name,
Showing their birth and where they did proceed?
O, know, sweet love, I always write of you,
And you and love are still my argument;
So all my best is dressing old words new,
Spending again what is already spent;
For as the sun is daily new and old,
So is my love, still telling what is told.

76

為什麼我的詩缺乏點睛之筆,

行文沉悶呆板,千篇一律?

為什麼我的詩不順應時尚,

花樣翻新,自鑄偉辭?

為什麼我總是重複同一個主旨,

我的所有詩趣總穿同一件詩衣?

幾乎每一個詞都打著我的印記,

透露它出自何手,意在何地何時。

啊,我的小親親,我的筆底明珠,

我只是寫你、寫愛、永遠不會換題。

竭聰盡智,我只能陳辭翻出新意境,

舊曲重彈,又何妨故技今日再重施。

  天上太陽,日日輪迴新成舊,

  銘心之愛,不盡衷腸訴無休。

Sonnet 77

Thy glass will show thee how thy beauties wear,
Thy dial how thy precious minutes waste,
The vacant leaves thy mind's imprint will bear,
And of this book this learning mayst thou taste:
The wrinkles which thy glass will truly show
Of mouthed graves will give thee memory;
Thou by thy dial's shady stealth mayst know
Time's thievish progress to eternity;
Look what thy memory cannot contain
Commit to these waste blanks, and thou shalt find
Those children nursed, delivered from thy brain,
To take a new acquaintance of thy mind.
These offices so oft thou wilt look
Shall profit thee and much enrich thy book.

77

鏡子會向你昭示衰減的風韻,
日晷會向你指出飛逝的青春,
這空白冊頁留有你心靈的軌跡,
你會從中細味妙諦相伴的人生。
鏡裡的皺紋絲絲,可數可辨,
讓你時時記得開口的墓門。
憑借日晷你心知星橫斗轉,
世間的腳步正蹣跚地走向永恆。
看,凡不能長駐你頭腦的東西,
都可以在這些空白的紙上留存。
你會看到你頭腦哺育出的兒女,
又再次魂交你自己的心靈。

　　你若能常對明鏡看日晷、寫心聲,
　　自會受益匪淺,這手冊也價值倍增。

Sonnet 78

So oft have I invoked thee for my Muse
And found such fair assistance in my verse
As every alien pen hath got my use,
And under thee their poesy disperse.
Thine eyes, that taught the dumb on high to sing
And heavy ignorance aloft to fly,
Have added feathers to the learned's wing
And given grace a double majesty.
Yet be most proud of that which I compile,
Whose influence is thine and born of thee.
In others' works thou dost but mend the style,
And arts with thy sweet graces graced be;
But thou art all my art, and dost advance
As high as learning my rude ignorance.

78

蒙你的垂顧我常得靈感的獎賞,
托你的蔭庇我這才詩心不僵。
於是另一些詩客群起而學步,
並借你的庇護使詩作傳揚。
你的雙眸曾教會啞子引吭歌唱,
曾教會沉重的無知在高空飛翔,
曾借來羽翼使學人雙翅生風,
曾賦予高士鴻儒威名遠蕩。
然而你引以為豪者是我的華章,
它們因你而生,全是你的兒郎。
對別人的詩作你只是改進其詩風,
有你的美質撐腰,他們才文采飛揚。
  但我的詩才不過是你詩魂的重現,
  是你讓我的粗陋昇華到博學高尚。

Sonnet 79

Whilst I alone did call upon thy aid
My verse alone had all thy gentle grace;
But now my gracious numbers are decayed,
And my sick Muse doth give another place.
I grant, sweet love, thy lovely argument
Deserves the travail of a worthier pen,
Yet what of thee thy poet doth invent
He robs thee of, and pays it thee again.
He lends thee virtue, and he stole that word
From thy behaviour; beauty doth he give,
And found it in thy cheek: he can afford
No praise to thee but what in thee doth live.
Then thank him not for that which he doth say,
Since what he owes thee, thou thyself dost pay.

79

我曾經獨自祈求獲得你的幫助,
我的詩也就獨自承蒙你高雅的惠顧;
可而今我筆下不再有繡句珍詞,
我那病繆斯只好把神龕拱手讓出。
甜愛啊,我承認你這個可親的題目
須有高人健筆縱橫、大書特書,
但描寫你的詩人儘管有筆下驚雷,
他不過是搶你又還你恰似物歸原主。
頌揚你的德,不過偷自你高尚的行為,
謳歌你的美,不過取自你雙頰的凝膚。
他不過把你原有的東西又還你本人,
離開你他的頌詞必然會語竭詞枯。
　　既然他付給你的無非是歸還舊帳,
　　那麼你對他的作為完全不必褒揚。

Sonnet 80

O, how I faint when I of you do write,
Knowing a better spirit doth use your name,
And in the praise thereof spends all his might,
To make me tongue-tied, speaking of your fame!
But since your worth, wide as the ocean is,
The humble as the proudest sail doth bear,
My saucy bark, inferior far to his,
On your broad main doth wilfully appear.
Your shallowest help will hold me up afloat
Whilst he upon your soundless deep doth ride;
Or, being wrecked, I am a worthless boat,
He of tall building and of goodly pride.
Then if he thrive and I be cast away,
The worst was this: my love was my decay.

80

啊,一面寫頌詩,一面滿懷淒涼,
因為另一名高手也在把你歌唱。
為了讚美你他不惜搜索枯腸,
要使我箝口結舌、頹筆無光。
但既然你的德行廣若四海,
當容得小船大舶共水同航;
我這輕舟雖萬難與其艨艟比量,
又何妨隨意駛進你海闊天長。
你有淺處可令我戲波其上,
亦有深處可供他縱馬鬆韁。
偶遇不測,我只是扁舟一葉不須惜,
他卻是巨艦宏舶,帆重桅高價高昂。
　　他日裡,假如是他得寵我遭放,
　　最壞不過此下場:我愛使我亡。

Sonnet 81

Or I shall live your epitaph to make,
Or you survive when I in earth am rotten.
From hence your memory death cannot take,
Although in me each part will be forgotten.
Your name from hence immortal life shall have,
Though I, once gone, to all the world must die.
The earth can yield me but a common grave
When you entombed in men's eyes shall lie.
Your monument shall be my gentle verse,
Which eyes not yet created shall o'er-read,
And tongues to be your being shall rehearse
When all the breathers of this world are dead.
You still shall live – such virtue hath my pen
Where breath most breathes, even in the mouths of men.

81

如你先我而逝我當寫下你的祭文,
如我不幸早衰便安然自朽於墓塋。
你縱然仙逝英名會長在人間,
我名賤身微當被人忘個乾淨。
你身雖歿有我的詩章使你長生,
我一旦辭別當永世化作微塵。
地闊天長,只賜我孤墳一處,
人心為塚,你在千萬人眼裡葬身。
我筆下詩行化作你墳前墓碑,
來日方長,自有人細續碑銘。
縱當今世界萬眾皆成厲鬼,
有千口萬舌對後世縷述你生平,
  凡有活人處你便活在人口,
  你與天齊壽,全仗我筆力千鈞。

Sonnet 82

I grant thou wert not married to my Muse,
And therefore mayst without attaint o'erlook
The dedicated words which writers use
Of their fair subject, blessing every book.
Thou art as fair in knowledge as in hue,
Finding thy worth a limit past my praise,
And therefore art enforced to seek anew
Some fresher stamp of the time-bettering days.
And do so, love; yet when they have devised
What strained touches rhetoric can lend,
Thou, truly fair, wert truly sympathized
In true plain words by thy true-telling friend;
And their gross painting might be better used
Where cheeks need blood: in thee it is abused.

82

我知你並非和我的詩神有過姻親,
因而你大可以披覽別人的詩文,
看他們如何為你舞文弄墨,
你不妨以讚許的恩威細斟慢評。
你兩全其美,不管是外表還是學問,
知我這禿筆難為你的大德寫真,
你因此不得不另請高明,
好將你在新時代的肖像更新。
好吧,我的愛,就這樣倒也成,
讓他們施朱著粉、辭藻用盡,
你那實在的美色只在我詩裡留存,
儘管我辭采淺淡,話兒卻說得真真。
　　他們的濃脂可使貧血臉生紅暈,
　　但對你的芳容卻簡直白費苦心。

Sonnet 83

I never saw that you did painting need,
And therefore to your fair no painting set.
I found – or thought I found – you did exceed
The barren tender of a poet's debt;
And therefore have I slept in your report:
That you yourself, being extant, well might show
How far a modern quill doth come too short,
Speaking of worth, what worth in you doth grow.
This silence for my sin you did impute,
Which shall be most my glory, being dumb;
For I impair not beauty, being mute,
When others would give life, and bring a tomb.
There lives more life in one of your fair eyes
Than both your poets can in praise devise.

83

從來不覺得你需要畫眉敷粉,
所以我從來不往你臉上貼金;
我發現或自以為發現你的風采
使詩人們報恩的頌詞更美妙十分。
於是我忙裡偷閒暫停把你歌唱,
好讓活生生的你把自己的美證明。
時下搖鵝毛管的人顯得多麼愚笨,
空嚷嚷你有美德卻愈說愈說不清。
你將我一時沉默看作是我的過錯,
其實我裝聾作啞更添我榮光數層。
因為我隱忍不發璧全你美色無雙,
他人欲錦上添花反害了卿卿性命。

　　你即使一隻眼眸也暗藏生機萬點,
　　遠勝我輩詩人,徒奉頌詞三千。

Sonnet 84

Who is it that says most which can say more
Than this rich praise: that you alone are you,
In whose confine immured is the store
Which should example where your equal grew?
Lean penury within that pen doth dwell
That to his subject lends not some small glory;
But he that writes of you, if he can tell
That you are you, so dignifies his story.
Let him but copy what in you is writ,
Not making worse what nature made so clear,
And such a counterpart shall fame his wit,
Making his style admired everywhere.
You to your beauteous blessings add a curse,
Being fond on praise, which makes your praises worse.

84

有誰能夠說出更美的頌詞

超過這一句:「只有你才是你」?

在誰的禁宮中有這樣一種寶庫,

會隨著你的寶貝漲縮合宜?

那一管筆中所藏真貧瘠無比,

難滴出些許鉛華賦贈它的母親。

惟那歌頌你者才能省識「你才是你」,

那他的詩威才能與你並駕齊驅。

且讓他只是把你當原稿抄錄,

別把造化結晶的成品損壞拋棄,

這樣一幅摹品會使它藝名鵲起,

普天下惟他的詩風所向披靡。

　　你該對你美麗的祝福加以詛咒,

　　愛聽恭維,恭維的價值就會降低。

Sonnet 85

My tongue-tied Muse in manners holds her still
While comments of your praise, richly compiled,
Reserve thy character with golden quill
And precious phrase by all the muses filed.
I think good thoughts whilst other write good words,
And like unlettered clerk still cry "Amen"
To every hymn that able spirit affords
In polished form of well-refined pen.
Hearing you praised I say " 'Tis so, 'tis true,'"
And to the most of praise add something more;
But that is in my thought, whose love to you,
Though words come hindmost, holds his rank before.
Then others for the breath of words respect,
Me for my dumb thoughts, speaking in effect.

85

我的繆斯緘口不語自有分寸,
其他詩人均為你歌唱,竭力嘶聲。
瞧他們奮筆揮灑下燦燦詩行,
分明是全體繆斯助其琢玉雕金。
我是信言不美,他們是美言不信,
他們有生花妙筆寫下積卷的頌文,
我恰似教堂裡領眾應答的白丁,
對才子的篇篇讚頌一口一聲「阿門」。
只要有人稱道你,我便說:不錯,當真,
即使頌詩已好到極點我還想金上添銀。
當然這只是我的想法,話兒尚未出口,
然而我的真愛卻早已領頭先行。
  那麼你且尊重他們,由於他們的雕章琢句;
  尊重我,由於我可意會而不可言傳的真情。

Sonnet 86

Was it the proud full sail of his great verse
Bound for the prize of all-too-precious you
That did my ripe thoughts in my brain inhearse,
Making their tomb the womb wherein they grew?
Was it his spirit, by spirits taught to write
Above a mortal pitch, that struck me dead?
No, neither he, nor his compeers by night
Giving him aid, my verse astonished.
He, nor that affable familiar ghost
Which nightly gulls him with intelligence,
As victors, of my silence cannot boast;
I was not sick of any fear from thence.
But when your countenance filled up his line,
Then lacked I matter; that enfeebled mine.

86

難道他的詩帆已長驅直入你的蒼溟，
先聲奪人俘獲了你價值連城的芳心？
可憐我情思萬種卻只能愁鎖腦際，
忍叫化育情思的子宮變作荒墳。
難道是他的詩心受鬼使神差
寫下超凡的詩句，令我落魄傷魂？
不，不是他，也不是夜半的精靈
曾助他一臂之力使我的詩思告罄。
他和那個伸出援手的和藹幽靈
都不能誇口曾星夜用智共舉奇兵，
遂使我情場敗北，無奈緘口稱臣，
因而我鎮靜自若，不詫也不心驚。
　　但當他的勁作直入你的心門，
　　我無門可進，軟搭搭沒了精神。

Sonnet 87

Farewell, thou art too dear for my possessing,
And like enough thou know'st thy estimate.
The charter of thy worth gives thee releasing;
My bonds in thee are all determinate.
For how do I hold thee but by thy granting,
And for that riches where is my deserving?
The cause of this fair gift in me is wanting,
And so my patent back again is swerving.
Thyself thou gav'st, thy own worth then not knowing,
Or me, to whom thou gav'st it, else mistaking;
So thy great gift, upon misprision growing,
Comes home again, on better judgement making.
Thus have I had thee as a dream doth flatter:
In sleep a king, but waking no such matter.

87

呵,再會吧,你實在是高不可攀,
而你對自己的身價也十分了然。
你德高望重到可不受拘束,
我們原訂的盟約就只好中斷。
沒有你的承諾我豈敢對你造次,
那樣的財寶我豈能輕動非分之念?
我既無堂皇的理由接受這份厚禮,
所以還請收回你給我的特許之權,
你當時自貴而不自知才以身相許,
錯愛了我,使我僥倖稱心如願。
判斷失誤,遂使你誤送大禮,
而今明斷再三,終得禮歸人還。

　　好一場春夢裡與你情深意濃,
　　夢裡王位在,醒覺萬事空。

Sonnet 88

When thou shalt be disposed to set me light
And place my merit in the eye of scorn,
Upon thy side against myself I'll fight,
And prove thee virtuous though thou art forsworn.
With mine own weakness being best acquainted,
Upon thy part I can set down a story
Of faults concealed wherein I am attainted,
That thou in losing me shall win much glory;
And I by this will be a gainer too;
For bending all my loving thoughts on thee,
The injuries that to myself I do,
Doing thee vantage, double-vantage me.
Such is my love, to thee I so belong,
That for thy right myself will bear all wrong.

88

有一天我或許在你心中一落千丈，
我過去的長處只贏得你輕慢的目光。
那時我當奮起反抗自己，
忘掉你的負心，證明你高尚。
對自己的缺點我最知內情，
為了你我可以編造撒謊，
說我內藏奸詐、人所不齒，
你失掉我的友誼，但贏得人們的讚揚。
我由此也將別有補償，
我雖然設計將自己損傷，
但既然我全部的愛心都在你身上，
傷我就保了你，保了你我也就沾光。
　　一切全屬於你，我的愛就是這樣，
　　只要為了你好，我情願蹈火赴湯。

Sonnet 89

Say that thou didst forsake me some fault,
And I will comment upon that offence;
Speak of my lameness, and I straight will halt,
Against thy reasons making no defence.
Thou canst not, love, disgrace me half so ill,
To set a form upon desired change,
As I'll myself disgrace, knowing thy will.
I will acquaintance strangle and look strange,
Be absent from thy walks, and in my tongue
Thy sweet beloved name no more shall dwell,
Lest I, too much profane, should do it wrong,
And haply of our old acquaintance tell.
For thee, against myself I'll vow debate;
For I must ne'er love him whom thou dost hate.

89

就說你對我負心是因為我自己有罪，
我願意對你的冒犯文過飾非；
說我腿瘸，我立刻蹦跳著行走，
對你給我的指摘絕不加以反對。
愛啊，如果你想造成體面的結局，
因而需要搞臭我自己的名聲，
與其你淤口相噴，不如我自辱其身。
我既已猜透你暗藏於胸的心事，
自會忍痛絕交，此後便形同路人。
躲開你，也不再提到你的芳名尊姓，
免得我過分褻瀆、傷害了它，
或不小心透露了我們舊有的交情。
　　為了你我發誓與自己來一場惡戰，
　　凡你所憎惡的人我絕不施一點愛心。

Sonnet 90

Then hate me when thou wilt, if ever, now,
Now while the world is bent my deeds to cross,
Join with the spite of fortune, make me bow,
And do not drop in for an after-loss.
Ah, do not, when my heart hath scaped this sorrow,
Come in the rearward of a conquered woe;
Give not a windy night a rainy morrow
To linger out a purposed overthrow.
If thou wilt leave me, do not leave me last,
When other petty griefs have done their spite,
But in the onset come; so shall I taste
At first the very worst of fortune's might,
And other strains of woe, which now seem woe,
Compared with loss of thee will not seem so.

90

你樂意恨我就恨我吧,立刻開始,
反正世人們現在都想和我為敵,
你可和厄運聯手強令我折腰,
別等我倒楣之時再落井下石。
啊別,當我的心已不再悲戚,
不要讓舊傷痕再添上憂思,
不要讓暴風夜續接黎明的急雨,
註定要來的厄運,何苦要延宕拖遲。
你如果要拋棄我,不要拖到最後,
不要讓我忍受春水長流般的輕愁,
要來就一齊來,也好讓我一開始
就把厄運最苦的滋味嘗個夠。
  其他各類憂傷儘管也像憂傷,
  但和失掉你相比不過小事一樁。

Sonnet 91

Some glory in their birth, some in their skill,
Some in their wealth, some in their body's force,
Some in their garments (though new-fangled ill),
Some in their hawks and hounds, some in their horse,
And every humour hath his adjunct pleasure
Wherein it finds a joy above the rest.
But these particulars are not my measure;
All these I better in one general best.
Thy love is better than high birth to me,
Richer than wealth, prouder than garments' cost,
Of more delight than hawks or horses be,
And having thee of all men's pride I boast,
Wretched in this alone; that thou mayst take
All this away, and me most wretched make.

91

有人因門第而貴，有人因才智而彰；
有人誇富比東海，有人詡力大無雙；
或忘形於華服，不自省其醜陋式樣；
或溺志於鷹犬，覺馬背上樂也泱泱。
人生各有其癖便自然各有其樂，
人人都認為己之所樂為萬樂之王。
可所有這一類快樂都非我的理想，
我將這一切快樂全都匯為一類！
你的愛對於我遠勝過高門大第，
勝過萬貫金銀，勝過華服奇妝，
比起鷹犬、比起馬更令我心醉，
只要有了你，我便是王中王。

  怕只怕生變故，你一旦出走，
    則萬事皆休，天下皆樂我獨愁。

Sonnet 92

But do thy worst to steal thyself away,
For term of life thou art assured mine,
And life no longer than thy love will stay,
For it depends upon that love of thine.
Then need I not to fear the worst of wrongs,
When in the least of them my life hath end.
I see a better state to me belongs
Than that which on thy humour doth depend.
Thou canst not vex me with inconstant mind,
Since that my life on thy revolt doth lie.
O, what a happy title do I find,
Happy to have thy love, happy to die!
But what's so blessed-fair that fears no blot?
Thou mayst be false, and yet I know it not.

92

但是你可以不辭而別鐵了寸心,
反正今生今世你已是我的人,
我的命不會長過你的愛,
因為是你的愛使我在世苟存。
既然你蹙眉就足以致我於死命,
我又何須惴惴不安於浩劫之來臨?
既然天堂之門可讓我駐足其內,
我又何須在世只看你的臉色生存?
既然你一變心我就小命不保,
我又何須自尋煩惱懼你覆雨翻雲?
哦,我找到多麼堂皇的享福的權利,
幸福地擁有你的愛,幸福地喪生!
　　但天下哪會有十全十美的事情,
　　我或許蒙在鼓裡不知你存有二心。

Sonnet 93

So shall I live supposing thou art true
Like a deceived husband; so love's face
May still seem love to me, though altered new
Thy looks with me, thy heart in other place.
For there can live no hatred in thine eye,
Therefore in that I cannot know thy change.
In many's looks the false heart's history
Is writ in moods and frowns and wrinkles strange;
But heaven in thy creation did decree
That in thy face sweet love should ever dwell;
What e'er thy thoughts or thy heart's workings be,
Thy looks should nothing thence but sweetness tell.
How like Eve's apple doth thy beauty grow
If thy sweet virtue answer not thy show!

93

那我還得像被騙的丈夫繼續生存,
假定你是忠實的,有脈脈溫情
雖今非昔比,似仍在你臉上停留,
只怕你目光看著我,心卻在比鄰。
既然你的眼睛不可能窩藏仇恨,
我又如何能猜透你已經變心?
有許多人臉上藏不住內心的變化,
皺眉、蹙額,每一神態都流露隱情。
但上天在造你的時候卻決定
教甜愛永遠在你臉上飄零。
無論你心中如何翻江倒海,
你總是表情甜蜜、神色若定。
 　假如你的德行和外表不那麼相稱,
 　你的美就和夏娃的蘋果甲乙難分。①

---

①典出《舊約‧聖經‧創世記》三章 6 節:伊甸園內長有外觀悅目而內藏邪惡的(智慧、知識)的蘋果。人類的祖先亞當和夏娃偷食後被上帝逐出伊甸園。

Sonnet 94

They that have power to hurt and will do none,
That do not do the thing they most do show,
Who moving others are themselves as stone,
Unmoved, cold, and to temptation slow
They rightly do inherit heaven's graces,
And husband nature's riches from expense;
They are the lords and owners of their faces,
Others but stewards of their excellence.
The summer's flower is to the summer sweet
Though to itself it only live and die,
But if that flower with base infection meet
The basest weed outbraves his dignity;
For sweetest things turn sourest by their deeds:
Lilies that fester smell far worse than weeds.

94

他們本有能耐害人卻沒有害人的心,
他們有很想做的事卻沒有做的閒情。
他們讓他者動心,自己卻磐石般安靜,
冷漠不動,視誘惑如怕火燒身。
惟他們能繼承上天的美質,
使造化的財產免消耗而長存;
他們是他們自己美貌的主宰,
別的人只是看護其美色的園丁。
夏日的花朵總把芬芳獻給夏日,
它們自己卻是吐盡香豔便凋零。
但是若花兒不幸染上了病毒,
那麼最卑賤的野草也比它高貴十分。
　　再香的東西一旦變質就臭不可聞,
　　百合花一旦腐朽就比野草還可恨。

Sonnet 95

How sweet and lovely dost thou make the shame
Which, like a canker in the fragrant rose,
Doth spot the beauty of thy budding name!
O, in what sweets dost thou thy sins enclose!
That tongue that tells the story of thy days,
Making lascivious comments on thy sport,
Cannot dispraise, but in a kind of praise,
Naming thy name, blesses an ill report.
O, what a mansion have those vices got
Which for their habitation chose out thee,
Where beauty's veil doth cover every blot
And all things turns to fair that eyes can see!
Take heed, dear heart, of this large privilege:
The hardest knife ill used doth lose his edge.

95

你讓羞恥變得多麼可愛清甜,
讓它像蟲兒深埋在玫瑰蕊兒中間,
使含苞欲放般的美名蒙上了污點,
呵,你簡直讓罪行戴上了柔美的花環!
那條專揭你個人隱私的不爛之舌
想對你的行為造出些猥褻的流言,
也不得不用讚美之詞來掩蓋其責難,
邪惡的話兒甜,因有你的美名作妝點,
啊,惡行所寄寓地方是一棟大廈,
這樣一座庇護之所真是稱它們心願,
在其中美的面紗遮住了每一個污點,
一切可見的事物都顯得美麗非凡。
　　小心呵,心肝,小心使用你這大特權,
　　再尖利的刀子,使濫了刃也會鈍殘。

Sonnet 96

Some say thy fault is youth, some wantonness;
Some say thy grace is youth and gently sport.
Both grace and faults are loved of more and less;
Thou mak'st faults graces that to thee resort.
As on the finger of a throned queen
The basest jewel will be well esteemed,
So are those errors that in thee are seen
To truths translated and for true things deemed.
How many lambs might the stern wolf betray
If like a lamb he could his looks translate!
How many gazers mightst thou lead away
If thou wouldst use the strength of all thy state!
But do not so: I love thee in such sort
As, thou being mine, mine is thy good report.

96

有人說你錯在年少浪蕩,
有人說你美在年少情長,
美和錯都多少受人讚賞,
你的過錯反使你美色增光。
就如同女王手上所戴的珠寶,
再粗劣也會受到人頌揚。
你身上的過失情形也一樣,
有人引為真理,有人為之捧場。
假如狼的猙獰換上了羊的溫馴,
多少羔羊將陷入惡狼的魔掌。
假如你一展你全部的風采,
多少人會為你魂飛魄蕩。
　　可你千萬別這樣,我的愛非比尋常,
　　我既然擁有你,也該擁有你的好名望。

Shakespeare's Sonnets

Sonnet 97

How like a winter hath my absence been
From thee, the pleasure of the fleeting year!
What freezings have I felt, what dark days seen!
What old December's bareness everywhere!
And yet this time removed was summer's time,
The teeming autumn big with rich increase.
Bearing the wanton burden of the prime
Like widowed wombs after their lords' decease.
Yet this abundant issue seemed to me
But hope of orphans and unfathered fruit,
For summer and his pleasures wait on thee,
And thou away, the very birds are mute;
Or if they sing, 'tis with so dull a cheer
That leaves look pale, dreading the winter's near.

97

你是這飛逝年華中的快樂與期盼,

一旦離開了你,日子便宛若冬寒。

瑟縮的冰冷攫住了我,天色多麼陰暗!

四望一片蕭疏,滿目是歲末的凋殘。

可是這離別的日子分明是在夏日,

或孕育著富饒充實的秋天,

浪蕩春情已經結下瑩瑩碩果,

好像良人的遺孀,胎動小腹圓。

然而這豐盈的果實在我眼中,

只是亡人的孤兒,無父的遺產。

夏天和夏天之樂都聽你支配,

你一旦離去,連小鳥也緘口不言。

　　它們即便啓開歌喉,只吐出聲聲哀怨,

　　使綠葉疑隆冬將至,愁色罩蒼顏。

Sonnet 98

From you have I been absent in the spring
When proud-pied April, dressed in all his trim,
Hath put a spirit of youth in everything,
That heavy Saturn laughed and leapt with him,
Yet nor the lays of birds nor the sweet smell
Of different flowers in odour and in hue
Could make me any summer's story tell,
Or from their proud lap pluck them where they grew;
Nor did I wonder at the lily's white,
Nor praise the deep vermilion in the rose.
They were but sweet, but figures of delight
Drawn after you, you pattern of all those;
Yet seemed it winter still, and, you away,
As with your shadow I with these did play.

98

是在春天的時候我就離開了你,
那時燦爛繽紛的四月披上了彩衣,
就連憂鬱的土星① 也含笑翩翩起舞,
呵,天下萬物處處都注滿了生機。
然而不管是百花鬥彩的撲鼻奇香,
也不管是悅耳醉人的鶯歌燕語,
都不能使我採摘下怒放的花兒,
或講述關於夏天的任何故事。
我也不企羨百合花的潔白,
也不讚嘆紅玫瑰的色豔香奇。
它們是你的摹品,有雅態濃香,
何敢與你這原型相匹,你萬美皆具。
於是我仍身處隆冬,只因你在異地,
我與這眾花嬉玩,若寄情於你的影子

---

① 憂鬱的土星:在星相學當中,土星象徵沉悶、憂鬱、衰老與死亡。

Sonnet 99

The forward violet thus did I chide:
Sweet thief, whence didst thou steal thy sweet that smells,
If not from my love's breath? The purple pride
Which on thy soft cheek for complexion dwells
In my love's veins thou hast too grossly dyed.
The lily I condemned for thy hand,
And buds of marjoram had stol'n thy hair;
The roses fearfully on thorns did stand,
One blushing shame, another white despair;
A third, nor red nor white, had stol'n of both.
And to his robb'ry had annexed thy breath;
But for his theft in pride of all his growth
A vengeful canker ate him up to death.
More flowers I noted, yet I none could see
But sweet or colour it had stol'n from thee.

99

我對早開的紫羅蘭頗有下面的微詞：
溫柔的賊，你若非沾漑於我愛人的氣息，
又何必偷得那奇香？殷紅淡紫
在你的柔頰上抹出流韻
全仗了我愛人的血脈染成。
我斥責薄荷花蕾取味於你的秀髮，
我斥責百合花盜用了你的晶瑩；
荊棘叢中的玫瑰慚然發抖，
白是你的絕望，紅是你的嬌羞，
不紅不白者，顯屬兩色兼取，
何止取色，連你的溫馨也偷。
卻不料得志的花兒如竊者當誅，
為復仇，花蟲咬斷了它的咽喉。
　　曾見過鮮花萬朵傲然怒放，
　　沒一朵不借你的秀色濃香。

Sonnet 100

Where art thou, Muse, that thou forget'st so long
To speak of that which gives thee all thy might?
Spend'st thou thy fury on some worthless song,
Dark'ning thy power to lend base subjects light?
Return, forgetful Muse, and straight redeem
In gentle numbers time so idly spent;
Sing to the ear that doth thy lays esteem
And gives thy pen both skill and argument.
Rise, resty Muse, my love's sweet face survey
If Time have any wrinkle graven there.
If any, be a satire to decay
And make Time's spoils despised everywhere.
Give my love fame faster than Time wastes life;
So, thou prevent'st his scythe and crooked knife.

100

繆斯,你在何方?為什麼許久以來
你沉默,竟把你力量的源泉忘懷。
你徒費狂放的詩情於陳詞濫調,
讓你的詩威屈尊於卑賤的題材,
歸來吧,健忘的詩神,年華已虛度,
何妨奏響壯歌一曲方不負詩才。
將你的歌唱傳向知音者的耳朵,
是他們賦予你的健筆主題和文采。
起來,慵睏的詩神,快端詳我愛的面龐,
看有否長溝橫渠在上面鋪排。
如果有,就寫下諷刺衰朽的詩句,
好讓時光的劫掠品處處無人睬。
　　快,趁我殘生未了,使我愛名遠揚,
　　我就再也不怕無常橫劍刈老除衰。

Sonnet 101

O truant Muse, what shall be thy amends
For thy neglect of truth in beauty dyed?
Both truth and beauty on my love depends;
So dost thou too, and therein dignified.
Make answer, Muse, wilt thou not haply say,
"Truth needs no colour with his colour fixed,
Beauty no pencil beauty's truth to lay,
But best is best if never intermixed"?
Because he needs no praise, wilt thou be dumb?
Excuse not silence so, for't lies in thee
To make him much outlive a gilded tomb,
And to be praised of ages yet to be.
Then do thy office, Muse; I teach thee how
To make him seem long hence as he shows now.

101

啊,詩神,有一種真侵染於美,
你卻不縱情謳歌,這又該當何罪?
真和美都仰仗我的愛而生存,
你也一樣,缺了它就無法稱作花魁。
回答吧,詩神,你幹嘛不說,
「真自有其色不必另外增輝,
美自有其真容何須借重畫筆,
天下至美,本不需雜色相隨。」
難道是因他不需讚詞你便乘機噤口,
別,別這樣沉默,須知你本有神威
讓他的英名留芳於千秋萬代,
縱然那時鍍金的墳墓已變為土灰。

　　那麼詩神,啓開歌喉吧,聽我的忠言,
　　讓他於百代之後,也照樣美譽滿天飛。

Sonnet 102

My love is strengthened, though more weak in seeming.
I love not less, though less the show appear.
That love is merchandized whose rich esteeming
The owner's tongue doth publish everywhere.
Our love was new and then but in the spring
When I was wont to greet it with my lays,
As Philomel in summer's front doth sing,
And stops her pipe in growth of riper days
Not that the summer is less pleasant now
Than when her mournful hymns did hush the night,
But that wild music burdens every bough,
And sweets grown common lose their dear delight.
Therefore like her I sometime hold my tongue,
Because I would not dull you with my song.

102

我的愛骨子裡已加強,外表上卻顯得弱,

我臉上雖顯淡漠,心裡卻熱戀如火。

愛既然不是商品,愛者的舌頭

就無需四處將其價值傳播。

想起我們的初戀,那時正值陽春,

我總是唱著歌兒去迎接愛的來臨,

有如夜鶯婉轉鳴啼於初夏,

要到夏末之時才停止歌吟。

不是說此刻的夏季不如當年愜意,

那時,他那哀傷之調曾使萬籟無聲。

我是說而今百鳥狂噪孤枝欲墜,

曲兒太多太俗,必失寵於心庭。

  因此,我學夜鶯,偶爾也緊閉雙唇,

  以免我用過多的曲兒使你煩心。

Sonnet 103

Alack, what poverty my Muse brings forth
That, having such a scope to show her pride,
The argument all bare is of more worth
Than when it hath my added praise beside.
O' blame me not if I no more can write!
Look in you glass and there appears a face
That overgoes my blunt invention quite,
Dulling my lines and doing me disgrace.
Were it not sinful then, striving to mend,
To mar the subject that before was well?
For to no other pass my verses tend
Than of your graces and your gifts to tell;
And more, much more than in my verse can sit,
Your own glass shows you, when you look in it.

103

唉,我的詩神本可乘機縱橫詩壇,
卻誰知到頭只寫出平庸的詩篇,
它的題材本身就價值無比,
有了我的頌詞卻貶值不如從前。
啊,如我不復寫作請別責難我,
照照鏡子吧,鏡中有一張臉蛋
遠遠超過我鈍拙的塗鴉之作,
狼藉了我的聲名使我詩趣大減。
好端端的題材反失於修修補補,
我茫然:自己是否已成了罪犯?
我的詩之為詩只為要頌揚你,
頌揚你博大的美德與才幹。

　　你有鏡子,照照你自己的鏡子吧,
　　我的歪詩所寫遠不如你鏡中所見。

Shakespeare's Sonnets

Sonnet 104

To me, fair friend, you never can be old;
For as you were when first your eye I eyed.
Such seems your beauty still. Three winters cold
Have from the forests shook three summers' pride;
Three beauteous springs to yellow autumn turned
In process of the seasons have I seen,
Three April perfumes in three hot Junes burned
Since first I saw you fresh, which yet are green.
Ah yet doth beauty, like a dial hand,
Steal from his figure and no pace perceived;
So your sweet hue, which methinks still doth stand,
Hath motion, and mine eye may be deceived
For fear of which, hear this, thou age unbred:
Ere you were born was beauty's summer dead.

104

俊朋友,我看你絕不會衰老,
自從第一次和你四眸相照,
你至今仍貌美如初。三冬之寒
已從疏林搖落三夏之妖嬈,
三度陽春曾轉眼化作金秋,
我曾踱過時序輪迴之橋,
看三回四月芳菲枯焦於六月,
而你仍鮮麗如昔似葉綠花嬌。
唉,嘆美色暗殞如時針流轉,
不見其動,卻已偷渡鐘面幾遭。
那麼你雖然貌似豔麗如舊,
或騙過我眼,暗地風韻漸消。
　　唉,不由我心焦,未來的時代聽我忠告,
　　你們尚未出世,美的夏天卻已死在今朝。

Sonnet 105

Let not my love be called idolatry,
Nor my beloved as an idol show,
Since all alike my songs and praises be
To one, of one, still such, and ever so.
Kind is my love today, tomorrow kind,
Still constant in a wondrous excellence.
Therefore my verse, to constancy confined,
One thing expressing, leaves out difference.
"Fair", "kind", and "true" is all my argument,
"Fair", "kind", and "true" varying to other words,
And in this change is my invention spent,
Three themes in one, which wondrous scope affords.
"Fair", "kind", and "true" have often lived alone,
Which three till now never kept seat in one.

105

不要說我的愛只是對偶像的崇敬，
也不要把我的愛說成祭壇上的天神，
儘管我所有的讚美歌都千篇一律，
唱之、頌之、今朝今日、來世來生，
善良是我今日的愛，明日也如此
有美倫妙質，越千古也常新。
所以我的歌只歌唱堅貞不渝，
長誦一個主題，哪怕千聲萬聲。
美、善、真，淘盡我胸中詩句，
美、善、真，概括我全部的詩魂。
縱橫衍變，耗盡我壯采奇思，
三題合一，直令人神往心馳。

　　美、善、真，從來獨立各擅其長，
　　只在今朝，喜見三長共體同彰。

Sonnet 106

When in the chronicle of wasted time
I see descriptions of the fairest wights,
And beauty making beautiful old rhyme
In praise of ladies dead and lovely knights;
Then in the blazon of sweet beauty's best,
Of hand, of foot, of lip, of eye, of brow,
I see their antique pen would have expressed
Even such a beauty as you master now.
So all their praises are but prophecies
Of this our time, all you prefiguring,
And for they looked but with divining eyes
They had not skill enough your worth to sing;
For we which now behold these present days
Have eyes to wonder, but lack tongues to praise.

106

曾翻閱過遠古史冊的零篇殘簡，
見往昔的美人留蹤於字裡行間，
古謠之美在於它謳歌的便是美，
絕色多情的佳人騎士都曾筆底生輝。
鏤句雕章，早寫盡天姿國色，
毫端翰墨臨摹盡手足眼唇及雙眉，
如椽的畫筆分明是想畫出美妙之身，
一如你今日展現的風采傾國傾城。
所以古往的一切讚詞都無非是預言，
預言我們這個時代，預言你的誕生。
因為古代詩人還只能想像你的風韻，
要歌頌你的價值還缺乏足夠的才情。
　　即便是我們，今日有幸親睹尊顏，
　　也只能望而興歎，恨無妙語驚人。

Sonnet 107

Not mine own fears nor the prophetic soul
Of the wide world dreaming on things to come
Can yet the lease of my true love control,
Supposed as forfeit to a confined doom.
The mortal moon hath her eclipse endured,
And the sad augurs mock their own presage;
Incertainties now crown themselves assured,
And peace proclaims olives of endless age.
Now with the drops of this most balmy time
My love looks fresh, and Death to me subscribes,
Since spite of him I'll live in this poor rhyme
While he insults o'er dull and speechless tribes;
And thou in this shalt find thy monument
When tyrants' crests and tombs of brass are spent.

107

無論是我自己的顧慮還是蒼茫乾坤

預知未來事物發展的先知之魂

都不能限制我的真愛的期限,

儘管有人認為愛終究化作荒墳,

人間的月亮已安然度過月蝕之災,①

曾預言不祥的人反成為笑柄。

疑慮叢生現轉變為信心百倍,

象徵和平的橄欖枝將永世長存。

今朝欣逢這盛事的甘露,我的愛

煥然一新,死神也對我俯首稱臣。

它雖會戰勝愚鈍無言的芸芸眾生,

卻奈何不了我,因為我能借歪詩活命。

  你也能憑我的詩行如堅碑長在,

  而暴君的勳徽與銅墓將化作埃塵。

---

① 國外莎學界有人認為,「人間的月亮」可能暗指伊莉莎白女王。西方人多以為,人的命運七年一個關口,63 歲為大關,1596 年,伊莉莎白女王度過其 63 歲大壽,故有學者認為此處暗示伊莉莎白女王已經平安無恙。

Sonnet 108

What's in the brain that ink may character
Which hath not figured to thee my true spirit?
What's new to speak, what now to register,
That may express my love or thy dear merit?
Nothing, sweet boy; but yet like prayers divine
I must each day say o'er the very same,
Counting no old thing old, thou mine, I thine,
Even as when first I hallowed thy fair name.
So that eternal love in love's fresh case
Weighs not the dust and injury of age,
Nor gives to necessary wrinkles place,
But makes antiquity for aye his page,
Finding the first conceit of love there bred
Where time and outward form would show it dead.

108

我的大腦裡的東西只要能成為筆底詩文,
有哪一樣不曾用來向你描述我的真心?
表達我的深愛,描摹你的美豔,
可憐聲音與文字再不能花樣翻新。
雖說如此,寶貝兒,我仍將日日夜夜
念經似的叨念同一篇愛的經文。
休說是老調重彈,你屬我,我屬你,
我說了又說,宛若當初敬頌你的芳名。
於是在簇新愛匣中的永恆之愛,
自能遠避年歲帶來的磨損與灰塵,
自能避免皺紋唐突擠佔一席之地,
好使暮年殘月永伴不死的青春。
　　儘管時光與外貌難遮愛的死相,
　　那最初的一縷愛葉卻永遠不會枯黃。

Sonnet 109

O, never say that I was false of heart,
Though absence seemed my flame to qualify
As easy might I from myself depart
As from my soul, which in thy breast doth lie.
That is my home of love. If I have ranged,
Like him that travels I return again,
Just to the time, not with the time exchanged,
So that myself bring water for my stain.
Never believe, though in my nature reigned
All frailties that besiege all kinds of blood,
That it could so preposterously be stained
To leave for nothing all thy sum of good;
For nothing this wide universe I call
Save thou, my rose, in it thou art my all.

109

啊,可千萬別說我假意虛情,
儘管別離似曾使我情火降溫,
我離不開自己如離不開自己的靈魂,
而我的靈魂卻在你的胸中紮根。
你的胸膛是我的愛的家園,如果
我曾像旅人浪跡天涯,今日回家門,
不遲不早,不因時而改變心身,
那我帶來了淨水好洗淨我罪惡的污痕。
儘管我的天性中有世人的一切弱點,
但請千萬不要相信我的性靈
會如此荒唐無稽到卑鄙,
竟至於無緣無故拋棄你這異寶奇珍。
  廣宇浩瀚對我來說一錢不值,
  只有你這玫瑰是我的凡塵命根。

Sonnet 110

Alas, 'tis true, I have gone here and there
And made myself a motley to the view,
Gored mine own thoughts, sold cheap what is most dear,
Made old offences of affections new.
Most true it is that I have looked on truth
Askance and strangely: but, by all above,
These blenches gave my heart another youth,
And worse essays proved thee my best of love.
Now all is done, have what shall have no end;
Mine appetite I never more will grind
On newer proof, to try an older friend,
A god in love, to whom I am confined.
Then give me welcome, next my heaven the best,
Even to thy pure and most most loving breast.

110

唉，我的確曾四海周遊，
做過當眾獻技的小丑，
自輕自賤，低價把最珍貴者出售。
為交新歡，不惜與舊友反目成仇。
千真萬確，我曾橫眉冷對忠貞，
但是，老天為證，我的荒唐不經
卻使我的心兒重溫韶華之夢，
不當的考驗證明你最值得我傾心。
一切都過去了，請接受這永恆之愛，
我將絕不再讓自己的欲火飛騰，
妄試新歡，以驗舊友情愫，
於我，舊情是牢籠我愛的天神。
　　那麼你這人間天堂，請將門大開，
　　讓我擁入你純潔至親的胸懷。

Sonnet 111

O, for my sake do you with Fortune chide,
The guilty goddess of my harmful deeds,
That did not better for my life provide
Than public means which public manners breeds.
Thence comes it that my name receives a brand,
And almost thence my nature is subdued
To what it works in, like the dyer's hand.
Pity me then, and wish I were renewed,
Whilst like a willing patient I will drink
Potions of eisel ' gainst my strong infection;
No bitterness that I will bitter think,
Nor double penance to correct correction.
Pity me then, dear friend, and I assure ye
Even that your pity is enough to cure me.

111

呵,但願你為了我而責難命運女神,

她是造致我行為不端的總根。

她不曾眷顧改善我的生活,

讓我隨俗謀生,舉止如同草野之民。

於是我的名字不免蒙羞,

我的天性的稜角也快磨平,

如染匠之手遇外色屈從於環境,

呵,可憐我吧,祝願我獲得新生,

我當如染病者甘心吞服下

一劑劑醋藥以治病防瘟。①

良藥再苦我也不覺得苦,

怕什麼雙重懲罰,但求改過自新。

  呵,可憐我吧,摯友親朋,請千萬相信,

  你的憐憫將使我從此不再病魔纏身。

---

① 伊莉莎白時代的人相信醋能防疫治病。

Sonnet 112

Your love and pity doth th'impression fill
Which vulgar scandal stamped upon my brow;
For what care I who calls me well or ill,
So you o'er-green my bad, my good allow?
You are my all the world, and I must strive
To know my shames and praises from your tongue
None else to me, nor I to none alive,
That my steeled sense or changes, right or wrong.
In so profound abyss I throw all care
Of others' voices that my adder's sense
To critic and to flatterer stopped are.
Mark how with my neglect I do dispense:
You are so strongly in my purpose bred
That all the world besides methinks are dead.

112

借得你的真愛和憐憫我當抹盡

流言的長舌在我額上烙下的污痕；

只要蒙你青眼相顧為我文過飾非，

我又何須在意對我說長道短的世人？

你既是我整個的世界，我必須

親耳聽到你對我的頌揚和批評。

我視世人皆亡，世人視我已死，

還有誰能以善惡改我鐵石之心？

我已把旁人的品頭論足都拋入

萬丈深坑，我像聾蛇充耳不聞[1]

惡意的誹謗或善意的奉承，

我這樣超然冷漠，本有原因：

> 你如此深深的紮根在我心底，
>
> 我想，除了你，全世界都已死去。

---

[1] 典出《舊約‧聖經‧詩篇》五十八篇 4-5 節：「他們塞著耳朵，像聾了的眼鏡蛇，聽不見弄蛇者的笛聲，也聽不見魔術師的喃喃咒語。」(聯合聖經公會，現代中文譯本)。

Sonnet 113

Since I left you, mine eye is in my mind,
And that which governs me to go about
Doth part his function and is partly blind,
Seems seeing, but effectually is out;
For it no form delivers to the heart
Of bird, of flower, or shape which it doth latch.
Of his quick objects hath the mind no part,
Nor his own vision holds what it doth catch;
For if it see the rud'st or gentlest sight,
The most sweet favour or deformed'st creature,
The mountain or the sea, the day or night,
The crow or dove, it shapes them to your feature.
Incapable of more, replete with you,
My most true mind thus makes mine eye untrue.

113

異地而處後,我的眼睛進入心庭,
從前是它指揮著我四處前行,
如今它形同半盲,不守職分,
雖睜大了眼皮,卻什麼也看不清。
花鳥或種種姿態明明在眼前飄過,
眼睛卻留不住形狀以便傳達給內心。
心兒無緣擁有那些過眼的物景,
眼兒無法把映入眼簾的東西留存,
無論見到的事物多麼粗俗、多麼雅致,
無論他們是多麼的美妙、多麼的畸形,
也無論他們是山、是海、是白天或黑夜,
是烏鴉或白鴿,眼睛總將其化作你的倩影。
 滿心裡裝著你,再容納不下其他事物,
 我這真誠的心兒就這樣使我變得盲目。

Sonnet 114

Or whether doth my mind, being crowned with you,
Drink up the monarch's plague, this flattery,
Or whether shall I say mine eye saith true,
And that your love taught it this alchemy,
To make of monsters and things indigest
Such cherubins as your sweet self resemble,
Creating every bad a perfect best
As fast as objects to his beams assemble?
O, 'tis the first, 'tis flatt'ry in my seeing,
And my great mind most kingly drinks it up.
Mine eye well knows what with his gust is 'greeing,
And to his palate doth prepare the cup.
If it be poisoned, 'tis the lesser sin
That mine eye loves it and doth first begin.

114

佔有了你我便富比王侯,是否我的心靈
便因此染上了帝王自我阿諛的瘟病?
不,或許我應該說,還是眼睛的話兒真?
因為你的愛使他們學會點石成金,
使妖魔也能化作天使般的嬰兒,
美貌溫存恰如同你的自身,
使天下目力所及的一切事物
縱然醜態,轉眼便美奐無倫。
哦,答案是前者,是眼睛的諂媚,
我這偉岸的心靈把它一口吞盡。
我的眼睛深知心靈的胃口,
所以按它的口味備下了杯羹:

  倘若杯羹中有毒,喝羹者罪也較輕,
  我的眼睛也喜歡它,早將味兒先品。

Sonnet 115

Those lines that I before have writ do lie,
Even those that said I could not love you dearer;
Yet then my judgement knew no reason why
My most full flame should afterwards burn clearer.
But reckoning Time, whose millioned accidents
Creep in 'twixt vows, and change decrees of kings,
Tan sacred beauty, blunt the sharp'st intents,
Divert strong minds to th' course of alt'ring things:
Alas, why, fearing of Time's tyranny,
Might I not then say "Now I love you best",
When I was certain o'er incertainty,
Crowning the present, doubting of the rest?
Love is a babe; then might I not say so,
To give full growth to that which still doth grow.

115

曾寫過說我愛你到極點的詩行，
我今兒卻要宣佈這些全都是謊。
可我那時的確說不出個道理，
為什麼日後我的情火會燒得更旺。
假如我當時想到千百萬次
時光會推翻盟誓，改變聖旨，
使絕色美人變黑，挫敗大略雄圖，
壯志凌雲終難改無常的時序，——
唉，懾於時間的暴戾專橫，
我那時幹嘛不說「我現在最最愛你」，
既然我那時已覺勝券在握，
雖知來日不可追，畢竟可使今朝喜？

　　愛是幼嬰；那時我的話不可能這樣，
　　為的是那成長中的嬰兒全面地成長。

Sonnet 116

Let me not to the marriage of true minds
Admit impediments. Love is not love
Which alters when it alteration finds,
Or bends with the remover to remove.
O no, it is an ever-fixed mark
That looks on tempests and is never shaken;
It is the star to every wand'ring barque,
Whose worth's unknown although his height be taken.
Love's not Time's fool, though rosy lips and cheeks
Within his bending sickle's compass come;
Love alters not with his brief hours and weeks,
But bears it out even to the edge of doom.
If this be error and upon me proved,
I never writ, nor no man ever loved.

116

呵,我絕不讓兩顆真心遇到障礙

難成百年之好。愛不是真愛,

如果對方轉彎自己立刻轉向,

如果對方變心自己立刻收場。

啊,不,愛應該是燈塔永遠為人導航,

雖直面暴風疾雨,絕不動搖晃蕩。

愛是星斗,指引著迷舟,

它的緯度可測,其價值卻難求。

儘管紅顏皓齒難逃過無常的鐮刀,

愛卻絕不是受時光愚弄的小丑。

滄桑輪迴,愛卻長生不改,

雄立千秋萬世直到末日的盡頭。

　　假如有人能證明我這話說得過火,

　　那就算我從未寫詩,世人從未愛過。

Sonnet 117

Accuse me thus: that I have scanted all
Wherein I should your great deserts repay,
Forgot upon your dearest love to call
Whereto all bonds do tie me day by day;
That I have frequent been with unknows minds,
And given to time your own dear-purchased right;
That I have hoisted sail to all the winds
Which should transport me farthest from your sight.
Book both my wilfulness and errors down,
And on just proof surmise accumulate;
Bring me within the level of your frown,
But shoot not at me in your wakened hate,
Since my appeal says I did strive to prove
The constancy and virtue of your love.

117

恨我、罵我吧,對你的大德恩威

我本應追思圖報,卻至今碌碌無為。

每天每夜我對你的至愛不曾稍減,

可我總是忘記讚頌你的深情和嫵媚。

我虛擲了你那千金難求的真情,

卻不惜屈尊結交無名之輩。

我張帆舉棹,任八面來風

吹送我離你遠渡海角邊陲。

現在請記下我的任性和錯誤,

好有足夠的鐵證將我合圍。

你大可以對我皺眉瞪眼,

萬不可盛怒之下叫我屍骨橫飛:

> 因為我的狀紙寫得分明,無非要證實:
> 你的愛真,真到今生無悔,百折不回。

Sonnet 118

Like as, to make our appetites more keen,
With eager compounds we our palate urge;
As to prevent our maladies unseen
We sicken to shun sickness when we purge:
Even so, being full of your ne'er-cloying sweetness,
To bitter sauces did I frame my feeding,
And, sick of welfare, found a kind of meetness
To be diseased ere that there was true needing.
Thus policy in love, t'anticipate
The ills that were not, grew to faults assured,
And brought to medicine a healthful state
Which, rank of goodness, would by ill be cured.
But thence I learn, and find the lesson true:
Drugs poison him that so fell sick of you.

118

正如為了有更好的胃口,

我們常用酸辣味刺激舌頭,——

我們服瀉藥用假病來把真病趕走。①

同樣吃夠了你那永不膩味的甘甜,

我轉而去把苦味的食物消受。

健康久了,就覺得生生病也好,

雖說本來就不必有這種需求。

愛的本意是要防止未發的疾病,

卻不料這種做法使疾病弄假成真:

好端端的身子卻偏要受罪於藥石,

原本是善的東西卻要讓惡來醫治。

  不過,我倒因此獲得了真正的開悟,

  誰要是厭倦了你,藥石也變成劇毒。

---

① 文藝復興時代的歐洲人常用瀉藥來預防疾病。瀉藥性烈,人飲後周身不適,如染疾病。

Sonnet 119

What potions have I drunk of Siren tears
Distilled from limbecks foul as hell within,
Applying fears to hopes and hlpes to fears,
Still losing when I saw myself to win!
What wretched errors hath my heart committed
Whilst it hath thought itself so blessed never!
How have mine eyes out of their spheres been fitted
In the distraction of this madding fever!
O benefit of ill! Now I find true
That better is by evil still made better,
And ruined love when it is built anew
Grows fairer than at first, more strong, far greater.
So I return rebuked to my content,
And gain by ills thrice more than I have spent.

119

曾喝過幾多賽倫女妖淚珠，①
它們像是從地獄般的蒸鍋裡蒸出——
使我把恐怖當救星，用希望醫治恐怖，
眼看勝利在望，卻總是敗績中途！
我的心在自以為最最幸福的時光
卻往往鑄下不堪再提的錯誤！
我曾經這樣地病狂到頭腦昏昏，
我的雙眼幾乎要奪眶而出！
哦，這就是惡的利端，我終於知道，
美好者可以因惡而更加美名昭著；
碎了的愛有朝一日破鏡重圓，
還可以比以前更美更強烈更突出。
　　所以我雖受譴責反而志得意滿，
　　由於惡我反倒可以三倍地因禍得福。

---

① 原文是 Siren tears，Siren 原為希臘神話中的女妖，慣以動人的歌聲引誘航海者觸礁，所以這一典故意味著女人之淚或致人於險境。

Sonnet 120

That you were once unkind befriends me now,
And for that sorrow which I then did feel
Needs must I under my transgression bow,
Unless my nerves were brass or hammered steel.
For if you were by my unkindness shaken
As I by yours, y'have pass'd a hell of time,
And I, a tyrant, have no leisure taken
To weigh how once I suffered in your crime.
O that our night of woe might have remembered
My deepest sense how hard true sorrow hits,
And soon to you as you to me then tendered
The humble salve which wounded bosoms fits!
But that your trespass now becomes a fee;
Mine ransoms yours, and yours must ransom me.

120

今日因禍得福於你過去對我的無情,
回首當初,我曾感到多麼傷心,
至今難以承受自己過失的重負,
因為我的神經畢竟不是鋼鐵鑄成。
假如我曾像你這樣對我無情相待
那你就會至今在煉獄裡棲身。
我這粗心的暴君竟從未偷空
把你對我傷害的程度加以權衡。
但願我們淒涼的夜晚還會記得
你殘酷的打擊深深刺傷了我的心靈,
我於是立刻仿效你向你奉獻歉意,
它如同藥膏可醫治你受傷的胸襟!
  你那時的過錯而今變成了補償,
  我的抵消你的錯誤,你的抵消我的罪行。

Sonnet 121

'Tis better to be vile than vile esteemed
When not to be receives reproach of being,
And the just pleasure lost, which is so deemed
Not by our feeling but by others' seeing.
For why should others' false adulterate eyes
Give salutation to my sportive blood?
Or on my frailties why are frailer spies,
Which in their wills count bad what I think good?
No, I am that I am, and they that level
At my abuses reckon up their own.
I may be straight, though they themselves be bevel;
By their rank thoughts my deeds must not be shown,
Unless this general evil they maintain:
All men are bad and in their badness reign.

121

冰清玉潔反蒙不辯的沉冤，
倒不如去作惡又不受惡名牽纏；
那種所謂合法之愛的快樂早已消失，
它徒投俗好，無視我們自身的情感。
為什麼別人的挑逗賣俏的目光
欲把我動盪不安的天性點燃？
為什麼更脆弱的人要窺視我的弱點，
我以為善者他們卻恣意稱為卑賤？
不，我就是我，任他們對我惡言相加，
不過是暴露他們自己的醜惡嘴臉。
他們可以彎腰駝背，我們卻要挺直腰桿，
他們齷齪的思想豈可把我們的行為評判！
　　除非他們堅信這樣一種異端：
　　全人類都是壞蛋，作惡是他們的本錢。

Sonnet 122

Thy gift, thy tables, are within my brain
Full charactered with lasting memory,
Which shall above that idle rank remain
Beyond all date, even to eternity;
Or at the least so long as brain and heart
Have faculty by nature to subsist,
Till each to razed oblivion yield his part
Of thee, thy record never can be missed.
That poor retention could not so much hold,
Nor need I tallies thy dear love to score;
Therefore to give them from me was I bold,
To trust those tables that receive thee more.
To keep an adjunct to remember thee
Were to import forgetfulness in me.

122

我心裡至今記著你送我的留言本，
其中的每一字每一行都寫得分明，
它們的品位高居一切留言贈語之上，
凌越千秋萬代，直到永恆，
或者至少延續到那麼一天，
當心和腦再也不能正常運行，
它們將徹底遺忘掉你的一切，
但是關於你的記錄仍將永遠留存。
可憐的筆記本容不下太多的東西，
我也不需別的手段來長保你的真情。
所以，我不再依靠你那本留言冊，
卻信託更有效的珍藏手段——我的心：
　　假使只有靠備忘錄才能記住你，
　　那麼這豈非暗示我是個健忘的人？

Sonnet 123

No! time, thou shalt not boast that I do change:
Thy pyramids built up with newer might
To me are nothing novel, nothing strange,
They are but dressings of a former sight.
Our dates are brief, and therefore we admire
What thou dost foist upon us that is old,
And rather make them born to our desire
Than think that we before have heard them told.
Thy registers and thee I both defy,
Not wond'ring at the present, nor the past;
For thy records and what we see doth lie,
Made more or less by thy continual haste.
This I do vow, and this shall ever be:
I will be true despite thy scythe and thee.

123

不！時光，休誇口說我也在隨你更新，
你縱有力量把金字塔重新建成，
對我而言，它們不新鮮、不稀奇，
頂多只不過是舊景換上了新衣。
世人一生的時間太短，所以你即使
給的是陳詞濫調，他們仍會豔羨不已，
認為那都是他們情之所鍾的東西，
卻不願意相信它們只是舊話重提
不論對你還是對我的記錄我一概排斥，
既不對現在表驚訝也不對過去表驚奇。
因你的記錄和我的觀察都不足為信，
都多少是你行色匆匆的餘痕。
  我現在立下重誓並且永無反悔，
  管你的鐮刀多鋒利我將萬古忠貞。

Sonnet 124

If my dear love were but the child of state
It might for Fortune's bastard be unfathered,
As subject to Time's love or to Time's hate,
Weeds among weeds or flowers with flowers gathered.
No, it was builded far from accident;
It suffers not in smiling pomp, nor falls
Under the blow of thralled discontent
Whereto th'inviting time our fashion calls.
If fears not policy, that heretic
Which works on leases of short-numbered hours,
But all alone stands hugely politic,
That it nor grows with heat nor drowns with showers.
To this I writness call the fools of Time,
Which die for goodness, who have lived for crime.

124

假如我的真愛只結胎於時勢和環境,

它就是命運的私生子,找不到父親,

或賤如野草,或躋身麗苑,

升沉冷暖只依靠與世浮沉。

哦,不,我的愛不會受機緣的影響,

它既不會因順境而反遭厄運,

也不會潦倒於憤世而積怨不平,

這種不平是流行於本朝的憂鬱病。

它不懼怕那些患得患失的弄權者,

恰如異教徒出租房屋賺取片時碎金。

不,它只是卓然鼎立,遠慮深謀,

不因驕陽而長,也不遭溺於雨淋。

  為我的話作證吧,為世所愛憎的癡人,

  你們或為善而死,或至今為惡而生。

Sonnet 125

Were't aught to me I bore the canopy,
With my extern the outward honouring,
Or laid great bases for eternity
Which proves more short than waste or ruining ?
Have I not seen dwellers on form and favour
Lose all and more by paying too much rent,
For compound sweet forgoing simple savour,
Pitiful thrivers in their gazing spent?
No, let me be obsequious in thy heart,
And take thou my oblation, poor but free,
Which is not mixed with seconds, knows no art
But mutual render, only me for thee.
Hence, thou suborned informer! A true soul
When most impeached stands least in thy control.

125

我高舉華蓋,想用外表來張揚
堂皇的門面,或是為所謂百世流芳
奠下偉大的根基,這一切有什麼用?
到頭來無非是更久的毀滅與荒涼。
難道我不曾目睹哪些租借表面排場的人
賠盡了血本仍敵不住租金的高昂?
厭倦了單調之味偏求雜拌濃湯,
窮困的富翁蕩產傾家只圖個表面輝煌。
不,讓我的忠誠在你的心中常保不衰,
收下吧,我這裡把綿薄的貢品奉上。
它只是我們之間推心置腹的贈禮,
毫不含次品雜質,可謂樸實無雙。
　　哦,你們這些誣告誹謗者,滾開吧,
　　真心似金,豈是你流言之火所能傷!

Sonnet 126

O thou my lovely boy, who in thy power
Dost hold Time's fickle glass, his sickle, hour;
Who hast by waning grown, and therein show'st
Thy lovers withering as thy sweet self grow'st
If Nature, sovereign mistress over wrack,
As thou goest onwards still will pluck thee back,
She keeps thee to this purpose: that her skill
May Time disgrace, and wretched minutes kill.
Yet fear her, O thou minion of her pleasure!
She may detain but not still keep her treasure.
Her audit, though delayed, answered must be,
And her quietus is to render thee.

126[①]

呵你,好男友,時間的鐮刀和沙漏

現在都已牢牢地受制於你的雙手,

時光的飛逝正反照出你在茁壯成長,

你的情人在凋零,你自己卻蒸蒸日上。

如果掌握生殺予奪大權的自然

把你從人生的路上往回驅趕,

那她只是為保存你而讓你看到

她的絕技能使時間倒流,擋住分秒。

你雖是她寵兒卻也會懼怕她的權威,

她能暫留卻不能長保其寵愛的寶貝。

　　她儘可以拖欠時光卻總歸會還清帳目,

　　　清償的日子一到,她只有把你交出。

[①] 此詩原作僅 12 行。一般莎評家認為此詩也是《莎士比亞十四行詩集》中致俊俏青年的最後一首詩。

Sonnet 127

In the old age black was not counted fair,
Or if it were, it bore not beauty's name;
But now is black beauty's successive heir,
And beauty slandered with a bastard shame:
For since each hand hath put on nature's power,
Fairing the foul with art's false borrowed face,
Sweet beauty hath no name, no holy bower,
But is profaned, if not lives in disgrace.
Therefore my mistress' eyes are raven black,
Her brow so suited, and they mourners seem
At such who, not born fair, no beauty lack,
Sland'ring creation with a false esteem.
Yet so they mourn, becoming of their woe,
That every tongue says beauty should look so.

127

從前，黑色絕不能與美並提，①

即使黑真正美也不能掛美的招牌。

而今黑色成了美的合法繼承者，

美受指責，由於它化育了雜種胎。

既然人人都暗借自然的威風，

用藝術的假面來為醜色美容，

自然美失掉名分，不再受人供奉，

即使不蒙羞，也會面對世人的不恭。

所以我的情人擁有烏黑的雙眉，

烏黑的眼睛，彷彿是黑衣追悼人

傷懷那些醜陋者，它們虛掛美名

欺世盜譽，令造化真容受損。

  然而他們渾然一體的哀容與哀心

  卻又眾口一詞：惟真美才如此相稱。

① 從此詩起到第 152 首，詩的主題涉及一位黑膚女人。

Sonnet 128

How oft, when thou, my music, music play'st
Upon that blessed wood whose motion sounds
With thy sweet fingers when thou gently sway'st
The wiry concord that mine ear confounds,
Do I envy those jacks that nimble leap
To kiss the tender inward of thy hand
Whilst my poor lips, which should that harvest reap,
At the wood's boldness by thee blushing stand.
To be so tickled they would change their state
And situation with those dancing chips
O'er whom thy fingers walk with gentle gait,
Making dead wood more blessed than living lips.
Since saucy jacks so happy are in this,
Give them thy fingers, me thy lips to kiss.

128

你是我的音樂,當你在幸運的琴鍵上
彈奏樂章,你輕柔的手指拂過鍵盤,
於是琴弦上隨指瀉出一串清響,
忍叫我雙耳聽了樂得發狂,
我常常多麼羨慕那些輕靈的琴鍵
跳蕩著親吻你柔嫩的指掌,
而我焦渴的嘴唇卻無緣竊玉偷香,
只能愧對大膽的琴鍵兀自羞立一旁。
心癢難熬,我但願自己的雙唇
能與歡跳的琴鍵易境換裝,
因為你輕盈的手指一旦掠過它們,
雖使枯木逢春卻使活唇淒涼。
　　既然放肆的琴鍵因此快樂無比,
　　給它們手指,我則把你的芳唇品嚐。

Sonnet 129

Th'expense of spirit in a waste of shame
Is lust in action; and till action, lust
Is perjured, murd'rous, bloody, full of blame,
Savage, extreme, rude, cruel, not to trust,
Enjoyed no sooner but despised straight,
Past reason hunted, and no sooner had
Past reason hated as a swallowed bait
On purpose laid to make the taker mad;
Mad in pursuit and in possession so,
Had, having, and in quest to have, extreme;
A bliss in proof and proved, a very woe;
Before, a joy proposed; behind, a dream.
All this the world well knows, yet none knows well
To shun the heaven that leads men to this hell.

129

損神，耗精，愧煞了浪子風流，

都只為縱欲眠花臥柳，

陰謀，好殺，賭假咒，壞事做到頭；

心毒手狠，野蠻粗暴，背信棄義不知羞。

才嘗得雲雨樂，轉眼意趣休。

捨命追求，一到手，沒來由

便厭膩個透。呀，恰像是釣鉤，

但吞香餌，管叫你六神無主不自由。

求時瘋狂，得時也瘋狂，

曾有，現有，還想有，要玩總玩不夠。

適才是甜頭，轉瞬成苦頭。

求歡同枕前，夢破雲雨後。

　　唉，普天下誰不知這般兒歹症候，

　　卻避不得偏往這通陰曹的天堂路兒上走！

Sonnet 130

My mistress' eyes are nothing like the sun;
Coral is far more red than her lips' red.
If snow be white, why then her breasts are dun;
If hairs be wires, black wires grow on her head.
I have seen roses damasked, red and white,
But no such roses see I in her cheeks;
And in some perfumes is there more delight
Than in the breath that from my mistress reeks.
I love to hear her speak, yet well I know
That music hath a far more pleasing sound.
I grant I never saw a goddess go:
My mistress when she walks treads on the ground.
And yet, by heaven, I think my love as rare
As any she belied with false compare.

130

我的情人眼睛絕不像太陽，

即便是珊瑚也遠比她的朱唇紅亮，

雪若算白，她的胸膛便算褐色蒼蒼，

若美髮是金絲，①她滿頭黑絲長。

曾見過似錦玫瑰紅白相間，

卻見不到她臉上有這樣的暈光；

有若干種香味叫人聞之欲醉，

我的情人嘴裡卻吐不出這樣的芬芳。

我喜歡聽她的聲音，但我明白

悅耳的音樂比她的更甜美鏗鏘。

我承認我從沒有見過仙女的步態，

反正我愛人只能在大地上徜徉。

  老天在上，儘管有所謂美女蓋世無雙，

  可我愛人和她們相比，卻也旗鼓相當。

---

① 當時詩人常以金絲喻女人的金髮，故有此說。

Sonnet 131

Thou art as tyrannous so as thou art
As those whose beauties proudly make them cruel,
For well thou know'st to my dear doting heart
Thou art the fairest and most precious jewel.
Yet, in good faith, some say that thee behold
Thy face hath not the power to make love groan.
To say they err I dare not be so bold,
Although I swear it to myself alone;
And, to be sure that is not false I swear,
A thousand groans but thinking on thy face
One on another's neck do witness bear
Thy black is fairest in my judgement's place.
In nothing art thou black save in thy deeds,
And thence this slander, as I think, proceeds.

131

有的人殘暴因為有美色作資本,
平庸如你,卻竟和她們一樣專橫;
只因為你知道我已愛迷了心竅,
總把你視作世上的至美奇珍。
可實話實説,凡見過你的都講,
你的臉還難以使人一往情深。
儘管我私下裡絕不信他們胡説,
可在公開場合卻不敢推翻他們的譏評。
我發誓我的話毫無半點欺心,
一想到你的嬌容,萬千嘆息
便不絕如縷湧出我口為我作證:
我看你的黑比天下絕色也不稍遜。

　　你其實一點不黑,黑的是你的驕橫,
　　我想是因為後者,誹謗才應運而生。

Sonnet 132

Thine eyes I love, and thy, as pitying me
Knowing thy heart torment me with disdain
Have put on black, and loving mourners be,
Looking with pretty ruth upon my pain;
And truly, not the morning sun of heaven
Better becomes the gray cheeks of the east,
Nor that full star that ushers in the even
Doth half that glory to the sober west,
As those two mourning eyes become thy face.
O, let it then as well beseem thy heart
To mourn for me, since mourning doth thee grace,
And suit thy pity like in every part.
Then will I swear beauty herself is black,
And all they foul that thy complexion lack.

132

我愛你的眼睛,他們知道你的內心

正輕蔑地折磨我,於是對我表同情,

便披上黑衫,宛若為癡情者哀悼,

睜大憐憫的眼,忍看我黯然魂傷。

長空的朝陽托出東方的魚肚色,

如天衣無縫,而暮色的黃昏星

也把清輝灑向浩浩空溟,待與

西天的殘霞平分入夜的寧靜,

但你淚眼的芳容比這一切更美,

哦,既然傷懷會使你美色倍增,

那就讓你的心也來為我哀悼,

好使憐憫與你全身如和弦交鳴。

　　那時我將發誓說美就是黑本身,

　　誰缺少了黑誰就是人間的醜人。

Sonnet 133

Beshrew that heart that makes my heart to groan
For that deep wound it gives my friend and me!
Is't not enough to torture me alone,
But slave to slavery my sweet'st friend must be?
Me from myself thy cruel eye hath taken,
And my next self thou harder hast engrossed.
Of him, myself, and thee I am forsaken
A torment thrice threefold thus to be crossed.
Prison my heart in thy steel bosom's ward,
But then my friend's heart let my poor heart bail;
Whoe'er keeps me, let my heart be his guard;
Thou canst not then use rigour in my jail.
And yet thou wilt; for I, being pent in thee,
Perforce am thine, and all that is in me.

133

我詛咒那一顆使我的心受傷的心,
它曾留給我和我的朋友深深的傷痕。
你本可以讓我獨自一人喝下苦酒,
又何必讓我的朋友同在你帳下充軍?
你那冷酷的雙眼已攝走我的魂兒,
現在又霸佔我的朋友,我第二個替身。
我已經不再屬於他、你和我自己,
於是對於我三重的痛苦就這樣降臨。
鎖我的心在你鐵石般的胸腔裡吧,
好讓我可憐的心保釋我朋友的心。
凡拘押我者我的心就是他的侍衛,
所以你縱教我入獄也無法對我專橫。

　　然而你畢竟要專橫,因為我植身於你;
　　我反正是你的,我的一切都是你的收成。

Sonnet 134

So, now I have confessed that he is thine,
And I myself am mortgaged to thy will,
Myself I'll forfeit, so that other mine
Thou wilt restore to be my comfort still.
But thou wilt not, nor he will not be free,
For thou art covetous, and he is kind.
He learned but surety-like to write for me
Under that bond that him as fast doth bind.
The statute of thy beauty thou wilt take,
Thou usurer that put'st forth all to use,
And sue a friend came debtor for my sake;
So him I lose through my unkind abuse.
Him have I lost; thou hast both him and me;
He pays the whole, and yet am I not free.

134

他是你的,這點我已經承認,
為填你的欲壑我成為你的抵押品。
心甘情願作你的俘虜,好讓另一個我
能被你釋放,我從而感到快樂舒心。
而你卻不能放他走,他也不想自由。
你雖縱欲無度,他倒也體諒溫存。
他本是為我作保,才在契約上簽字,
卻誰知那契約反把他箍得緊緊。
你的美貌使你能得到特權
隨心所欲地使用你的抵押品,
我的朋友也因我而成為你的債務人,
我連累和失去了他,你的控訴得逞。

  我不再擁有他,你卻把我們兩個抓牢,
  他了清舊債,我卻不能自在逍遙。

Sonnet 135

Whoever hath her wish, thou hast thy Will,
And Will to boot, and Will in overplus.
More than enough am I that vex thee still,
To thy sweet will making addition thus.
Wilt thou, whose will is large and spacious,
Not once vouchsafe to hide my will in thine?
Shall will in others seem right gracious,
And in my will no fair acceptance shine?
The sea, all water, yet receives rain still,
And in abundance addeth to his store;
So thou, being rich in Will, add to thy Will
One will of mine to make thy large Will more,
Let no unkind no fair beseechers kill;
Think all but one, and me in that one Will.

135

只要她有心欲你就會有意欲，①
多重的欲、多量的欲、多餘的欲；
我是那總攪得你心神不寧的人，
想把過量的欲火放進你的欲池。
你的欲界既如此大度寬廣，
何不賞臉讓我偷偷進去一次？
難道別人的意欲就那麼逗人喜愛，
獨獨我的意欲難蒙你的蔭庇？
大海本來就滿是水還照樣接受雨水，
好使它的水更加汪洋恣肆；
你的意欲雖多，又何妨添進我的，
好擴大你的欲界使得你欲海無際？
　　別，別無情拒絕求愛的風流種，
　　想萬欲無非是欲，我的欲有甚不同？

---

① 此詩及 133 首和 136 首均不同程度地圍繞 will（意欲，意志）一字做文字遊戲，色情味甚濃。will 可作數解：1)意志；2)欲望；3)男性陽具；4)女性陰道；5)威廉·莎士比亞的威廉(william)的暱稱。

Sonnet 136

If thy soul check thee that I come so near,
Swear to thy blind soul that I was thy Will,
And will, thy soul knows, is admitted there;
Thus far for love my love-suit, sweet, fulfil.
Will will fulfil the treasure of thy love,
Ay, fill it full with wills, and my will one.
In things of great receipt with ease we prove
Among a number one is reckoned none.
Then in the number let me pass untold,
Though in thy store's account I one must be;
For nothing hold me, so it please thee hold
That nothing me, a something sweet to thee.
Make but my name thy love, and love that still,
And then thou lov'st me for my name is Will.

136

若你的靈魂罵我貼你貼得太親密,
那就對瞎眼靈魂說我原是你的心欲;
你的魂兒知道心欲理當在此,
為了愛且讓我的心欲有圓滿的甜蜜。
我這愛欲將填塞你愛的寶庫,
唉,除了我的欲這寶庫還充斥別的欲,
說到大容器我們憑經驗可知,
裝得多了,添一個就不算稀奇。
那麼讓我不計入總數地進去吧,
但記住我這欲理應在你庫存單裡。
我的誠然渺小,只望蒙你錯愛收留,
雖微賤畢竟於你柔情不減如膠似漆。
  將我的欲名當你的愛,愛它一世一生,
  我的名就是心欲,愛它就是愛鄙人。

Shakespeare's Sonnets

Sonnet 137

Thou blind fool, Love, what dost thou to mine eyes,
That they behold and see not what they see ?
They know what beauty is, see where it lies,
Yet what the best is take the worst to be.
If eyes corrupt by over-partial looks,
Be anchored in the bay where all men ride,
Why of eyes' falsehood hast thou forged hooks
Whereto the judgement of my heart is tied?
Why should my heart think that a several plot
Which my heart knows the wide world's common place?
Or mine eyes seeing this, say this is not,
To put fair truth upon so foul a face?
In things right true my heart and eyes have erred,
And to this false plague are they now transferred.

137

愛啊，瞎眼的蠢貨，你幹了什麼
使我看不見東西儘管我雙眼大睜？
我的眼明知道美是什麼，住在何處，
卻偏偏把極善錯當作了極惡。
如果眼睛受過度的偏見迷惑，
在所有男人愛停靠的港灣裡停泊，
你又為何鍛造出虛偽眼睛的錨鉤，
緊緊鉤住我心靈判斷的寓所？
為何我的心仍把那港灣看作私有地產，
儘管明知人人可在那裡拋錨駛舵？
為何我的眼明明看見了這一切
卻漠然而讓醜臉圍上真美的綾羅？
　　我的心和眼在真假是非上犯了錯，
　　所以現在只好受虛情假意的折磨。

Sonnet 138

When my love swears that she is made of truth
I do believe her though I know she lies,
That she might think me some untutored youth
Unlearned in the world's false subtleties.
Thus vainly thinking that she thinks me young,
Although she knows my days are past the best,
Simply I credit her false-speaking tongue;
On both sides thus is simple truth suppressed.
But wherefore says she not she is unjust,
And wherefore say not I that I am old?
O, love's best habit is in seeming trust,
And age in love loves not to have years told.
Therefore I lie with her, and she with me,
And in our faults by lies we flattered be.

138

我的愛賭咒發誓說她遍體忠誠，
我明知此語有假卻樂得信以為真；
這樣她就會認為我是不曉事的孩子，
對世間的一切騙局從不存戒心。
我於是會玄想她還以為我年少，
雖然她知道我早已過青春妙齡。
我傻呼呼地相信她的胡編亂造，
這一來我和她都在隱瞞真情。
然而她為何不說她話中有假？
為何我不說我已經老邁無能？
唉，愛的堂皇服裝是表面忠貞，
年歲大的人最不喜把年齡談論。

  於是我糊弄了她，她也糊弄了我，
  我們互相糊弄，樂在騙裡縱情。

Sonnet 139

O, call not me to justify the wrong
That thy unkindness lays upon my heart.
Wound me not with thine eye but with thy tongue;
Use power with power, and slay me not by art.
Tell me thou lov'st elsewhere, but in my sight,
Dear heart, forbear to glance thine eye aside.
What need'st thou wound with cunning when thy might
Is more than my o'erpressed defence can bide?
Let me excuse thee: ah, my love well knows
Her pretty looks have been mine enemies,
And therefore from my face she turns my foes
That they elsewhere might dart their injuries.
Yet do not so; but since I am near slain,
Kill me outright with looks, and rid my pain.

139

你曾殘忍地傷害過我的心,

那麼別指望我諒解你的暴行,

請用舌頭傷我,可別用你的眼睛,

剷殺隨你,要公開,別使小聰明。

呵,心肝,你不妨直說你芳心已改,

萬不要當我面與別人眉目傳情。

要傷我你毋須巧取,我勢單力薄,

怎擋得住你心藏百萬雄兵?

讓我來為你辯護吧,唉,我的愛知曉

那流盼的目光是我的敵人,

於是她別轉臉蛋將敵陣他引,

好使別處遭受兵災的摧凌。

  可是別,別這樣,反正我已行將就木,

  你就用目光殺我吧,幫我把苦痛根除。

Sonnet 140

Be wise as thou art cruel; do not press
My tongue-tied patience with too much disdain,
Lest sorrow lend me words, and words express
The manner of my pity-wanting pain.
If I might teach thee wit, better it were,
Though not to love, yet, love to tell me so
As testy sick men, when their deaths be near
No news but health from their physicians know.
For if I should despair I should grow mad,
And in my madness might speak ill of thee.
Now this ill-wresting world is grown so bad
Mad slanderers by mad ears believed be.
That I may not be so, nor thou belied,
Bear thine eyes straight, though thy proud heart go wide.

140

當心啊，你可別一味由著性兒殘酷，
我緘口的忍耐或難容你過份的侮辱，
到時候悲哀會化作言辭，如衷曲
述説我心中失掉你哀憐的痛苦。
如果我能教會你學乖，那麼，
你就會言不由衷地説你還愛我如初。
這就像脾氣不好的病人，雖近死期，
仍一味要醫生説，他會很快康復。
因為，我如果不幸於絕望中瘋狂，
就可能在狂戀裡亂揭你的陰私和錯誤。
而今這附逆助惡的世界已壞到了頭，
瘋耳朵偏能與瘋謊言和睦相處。
　　要我不瘋狂，你也不遭到誹謗，
　　你要正眼看人，縱心裡男盜女娼。

Shakespeare's Sonnets

Sonnet 141

In faith, I do not love thee with mine eyes,
For they in thee a thousand errors note;
But 'tis my heart that loves what they despise,
Who in despite of view is pleased to dote.
Nor are mine ears with thy tongue's tune delighted,
Nor tender feeling to base touches prone;
Nor taste, nor smell, desire to be invited
To any sensual feast with thee alone;
But my five wits nor my five senses can
Dissuade one foolish heart from serving thee,
Who leaves unswayed the likeness of a man,
Thy proud heart's slave and vassal wretch to be.
Only my plague thus far I count my gain:
That she that makes me sin awards me pain.

141

說真的,我愛你並不借助於我的眼睛,

因為眼睛看到你身上處處是毛病,

不過眼睛所輕視的東西,心卻在愛,

心兒不管目之所見,只是愛意日深。

我的耳朵聽不見你吟誦的歌曲,

我敏感的觸覺無興致撫摸你的肉身。

還有味覺和嗅覺都變得麻木,

不願單獨得樂趣於你的肉體官能。

然而我的五種心智和五種感官,

都擋不住我的癡心來膜拜你的榴裙。

我現在徒有人形,六神無主,

只默然臣服於你傲慢的心靈。

　　不過我這愛的瘟病也自有其好處:
　　我犯罪的同時可領略贖罪的痛苦。

Sonnet 142

Love is my sin, and thy dear virtue hate,
Hate of my sin grounded on sinful loving.
O, but with mine compare thou thine own state,
And thou shalt find it merits not reproving;
Or if it do, not from those lips of thine
That have profaned their scarlet ornaments
And sealed false bonds of love as oft as mine,
Robbed others' beds' revenues of their rents.
Be it lawful I love thee as thou lov'st those
Whom thine eyes woo as mine importune thee.
Root pity in thy heart, that when it grows
Thy pity may deserve to pitied be.
If thou dost seek to have what thou dost hide,
By self-example mayst thou be denied.

142

愛是我的罪惡,恨則是我的德行,

因為你恨的是我的有罪的愛情。

但是如果比較一下你我的處境,

你就會發現你的恨有點過份。

就算你該恨,也不該淤了尊口,

你唇邊的口紅已橫遭侵凌,

一如從前對我,虛蓋上愛的假印,

曾於他人的枕畔背著我盜玉偷金。

我愛你就跟你愛他們一樣合法,

我的眼睛纏著你,你的垂涎著他們。

向你的心中注滿善良的慈悲吧,

你可憐我你也會交上被可憐的運。

  假如你希求憐憫卻藏起自己的慈悲,

  別人也就會學你的樣子對你橫眉冷對。

Shakespeare's Sonnets

Sonnet 143

Lo, as a careful housewife runs to catch
One of her feathered creatures broke away,
Sets down her babe and makes all swift dispatch
In pursuit of the thing she would have stay,
Whilst her neglected child holds her in chase,
Cries to catch her whose busy care is bent
To follow that which flies before her face,
Not prizing her poor infant's discontent:
So run'st thou after that which flies from thee,
Whilst I, thy babe, chase thee afar behind;
But if thou catch thy hope, turn back to me
And play the mother's part: kiss me, be kind.
So will I pray that thou mayst have thy Will
If thou turn back and my loud crying still.

143

看呀,當一隻家禽跑出了圍欄,
細心的主婦拔腿便去追趕,
她放下了孩子,飛奔而去,
緊緊追著她想得到的心肝。
她那沒人照管的孩子則隨蹤其後,
嚷叫哀號,而她卻一門心思衝向前,
窮追不捨從眼底逃掉的雄雞,
毫不理睬孩子可憐的哭喊。
我也是你的兒童,遠循著你的行蹤,
你呢,也在追逐離你而去的負心漢,
求你一旦抓住了心願,便回身向我,
作一個好媽媽,吻我,對我慈善。
  呵,只要你回過身來止住我的悲鳴,
  我就會祝願你,讓你快活無限。

Sonnet 144

Two loves I have, of comfort and despair,
Which like two spirits do suggest me still.
The better angel is a man right fair,
The worser spirit a woman coloured ill.
To win me soon to hell my female evil
Tempteth my better angel from my side,
And would corrupt my saint to be a devil,
Wooing his purity with her foul pride;
And whether that my angel be turned fiend
Suspect I may, yet not directly tell;
But being both from me, both to each friend,
I guess one angel in another's hell.
Yet this shall I ne'er know, but live in doubt
Till my bad angel fire my good one out.

144

我有兩個愛人,分管著安慰和絕望,
像兩個精靈,輪番誘惑在我的心房,
善的那一個是男人,英俊瀟灑,
惡的那一個是女人,臉黑睛黃。
為使我早日跨進絕望的地獄,
邪惡陰柔騙走了我善性的陽剛,
她還使我的好精靈化作魔鬼,
用髒污的肉慾使其純真淪為荒唐。
我的善精神是否已成妖魅,我疑心,
卻不能立刻有一個蓋棺論定,
但既然這兩人都離我朋比為奸,
我敢說善精靈已進了另一個的陰間門。

 除了瞎猜我永不知那葫蘆裝的什麼藥,
 除非是惡精靈用梅毒把善精靈嚇跑。

Sonnet 145

Those lips that Love's own hand make
Breathed forth the sound that said "I hate"
To me that languished for her sake;
But when she saw my woeful state,
Straight in her heart did mercy come,
Chiding that tongue that ever sweet
Was used in giving gentle doom,
And taught it thus anew to greet:
"I hate" she altered with an end
That followed it as gentle day
Doth follow night, who like a fiend,
From heaven to hell is flown away.
"I hate" from hate away she threw,
And saved my life, saying "not you."

145

為愛神我黯然傷神,
而她卻用親自造成的雙唇
對我吐出了一聲「我恨」。
但當她看到我悲哀的處境,
便立刻滿懷慈悲之心,
責備舌頭一改舊時的甜蜜溫存,
雖拒絕也應措辭委婉,
所以須對我客氣三分:
「我恨」,她未説完便中途停下,
這一停頓便迎來氣朗天清,
先前的暗夜有如魔鬼,
從天堂被扔進地獄之門。
　　她把「我恨」的「恨」字拋棄,
　　補一句「不是你」便救了我的命。

Sonnet 146

Poor soul, the centre of my sinful earth,
[....] these rebel powers that thee array;
Why dost thou pine within and suffer dearth,
Painting thy outward walls so costly gay?
Why so large cost, having so short a lease,
Dost thou upon thy fading mansion spend?
Shall worms, inheritors of this excess,
Eat up thy charge? Is this thy body's end?
Then, soul, live thou upon thy servant's loss,
And let that pine to aggravate thy store.
Buy terms divine in selling hours of dross;
Within be fed, without be rich no more.
So shalt thou feed on Death, that feeds on men,
And Death once dead, there's no more dying then.

146

可憐的靈魂，罪惡軀體的中心，
反叛的情欲纏繞著你全身，
為什麼你這樣深心裡強忍饑寒，
卻又竭力在軀殼上塗脂抹粉？
人生苦短，你又何須憐惜這副臭皮囊，
為它花盡你庫藏的金銀？
到頭來，無非是屍蟲承繼你的豪奢，
饕餮你的貴體，敢問皮囊安存？
靈魂啊，你何妨借軀殼的損耗而偷生，
他會瘦，但卻增加你庫內的收成：
用時間的碎銀買進永生，
休管那堂堂儀表，只要能餵飽靈魂。
　　於是你將吃掉以人為食的死神，
　　死神一死，世上就不再有死亡發生。

Sonnet 147

My love is as a fever, longing still
For that which longer nurseth the disease,
Feeding on that which doth preserve the ill,
Th' uncertain sickly appetite to please.
My reason, the physician to my love,
Angry that this prescriptions are not kept,
Hath left me, and I desperate now approve
Desire is death, which physic did except.
Past cure I am, now reason is past care,
And frantic mad with evermore unrest.
My thoughts and my discourse as madmen's are,
At random from the truth vainly expressed;
For I have sworn thee fair, and thought thee bright,
Who art as black as hell, as dark as night.

147

我的愛是熱病,它永遠在渴望

能使其熱狀態總呈高潮的藥方,

它總在吞吃那增熱延病之物,

使它那翻雲覆雨的肉欲如願以償。

我的理智(根治我熱戀病的醫生)

勃然大怒,因我將其處方擱置一旁。

理智離開了我,我這才痛苦地明白:

諱疾忌醫的欲望本身就是死亡。

理智扔下了我,我只能病入膏肓,

終日裡煩躁不安、幾近瘋狂,

言談思緒有如癲子一般,

連篇的胡話掩蓋了真相。

  可憐我曾堅信你美色光彩燦爛,

  到頭來你卻暗若夜晚、黑如陰間。

Sonnet 148

O me! what eyes hath Love put in my head,
Which have no correspondence with true sight,
Or if they have, where is my judgement fled,
That censures falsely what they see aright?
If that be fair whereon my fales eyes dote,
What means the world to say it is not so?
If it be not, then love doth well denote
Love's eye is not so true as all men's: no,
How can it, O, how can Love's eye be true,
That is so vexed with watching and with tears?
No marvel then though I mistake my view:
The sun itself sees not till heaven clears.
O cunning Love, with tears thou keep'st me blind
Lest eyes well seeing thy foul faults should find.

148

啊,天!愛在我頭上安的什麼眼?[1]
為什麼它面對真相視而不見?
說看得見吧,我的判斷力又在何方?
何以眼睛看得見對它卻一片茫然?
如果使我的眼迷戀的東西真是美景,
如何世人偏要說它醜陋難堪?
如果所見不美,那我的愛戀等於說:
愛情之眼實不如常人之眼健全。
是呀,它不美能健全得了嗎?
你瞧它強睜淚眼徹夜不眠。
這麼說我看不清景象不算稀罕,
就是太陽也須晴日才光照塵寰。
  啊,狡詐的愛,你用淚水遮住我的視線,
  只怕亮眼會把你醜陋的真相看穿。

---

[1] 關於頭(head),莎氏有許多隱喻,散見於其劇作中,常具有性暗示。參見莎劇《羅密歐與茱麗葉》第一幕第一場。

Sonnet 149

Canst thou, O cruel, say I love thee not
When I against myself with thee partake?
Do I not think on thee when I forgot
Am of myself, all tyrant, for thy sake?
Who hateth thee that I do call my friend?
On whom frown'st thou that I do fawn upon?
Nay, if thou low'r'st on me, do I not spend
Revenge upon myself with present moan?
What merit do I in myself respect
That is so proud thy service to despise,
When all my best doth worship thy defect,
Commanded by the motion of thine eyes?
But, love, hate on, for now I know thy mind.
Those that can see thou lov'st, and I am blind.

149

死冤家，你怎能説我對你沒真情？

要知道我的自我作踐只是要討你的歡心，

呵，你這天殺的，我為你得了相思病，

全忘了自己也是一個人。

難道我曾認敵為友和你作對？

難道我曾曲意奉承你的眼中釘？

你只要對我略表厭惡，我立刻領情，

愁眉苦臉地把我自己憎恨。

你流轉的秋波使我欲效犬馬之忠，

你的缺陷也叫我的美德崇拜銷魂。

我身上豈能還有至美大善，

可使我睥睨萬物而不對你拱手稱臣？

　　啊，愛啊，你恨吧，我現在已看透你的心，

　　你只愛能看清真相者，而我卻是盲人。

Sonnet 150

O, from what power hast thou this powerful might
With insufficiency my heart to sway,
To make me give the lie to my true sight
And swear that brightness doth not grace the day?
Whence hast thou this becoming of things ill,
That in the very refuse of thy deeds
There is such strength and warrantise of skill
That in my mind thy worst all best exceeds?
Who taught thee how to make me love thee more
The more I hear and see just cause of hate?
O, though I love what others do abhor,
With others thou shouldst not abhor my state.
If thy unworthiness raised love in me,
More worthy I to be beloved of thee.

150

啊,你那魔力究竟來自什麼源泉,

竟能左右我的心靈,儘管你有缺陷?

你教我把眼見為實稱作謊言,

強要我承認黑夜就是白天。

你在何處練成點石成金般的本事,

可使你的醜行惡狀獲得遮掩,

並能顯示出你智慧無比、威力非凡,

讓你的至惡也能勝過我心中的至善。

儘管我所見所聞裡你醜行醜態日多,

是誰授你秘方讓我愛意更纏綿?

即便我之所愛恰是他人所憎,

你不該同他人一道來把我怨嫌。

　　假如你的缺陷也曾激起我的愛泉,

　　那麼愛你並被你愛就更值得稱讚。

Sonnet 151

Love is too young to know what conscience is,
Yet who knows not conscience is born of love?
Then, gentle cheater, urge not my amiss,
Lest guilty of my faults thy sweet self prove.
For, thou betraying me, I do betray
My nobler part to my gross body's treason.
My soul doth tell my body that he may
Triumph in love; flesh stays no farther reason,
But rising at thy name doth point out thee
As his triumphant prize. Proud of this pride,
He is contented thy poor drudge to be,
To stand in thy affairs, fall by thy side.
No want of conscience hold it that I call
Her "love" for whose dear love I rise and fall.

151

雖説愛神太幼小，不懂得什麼叫良心，①
可是誰不知良心原是愛心所生？
那麼溫柔的騙子你可別揪住我的錯處，
謹防它成為你也曾犯罪的鐵證。
因為你騙了我，我也與粗鄙肉體聯手
騙我那更高貴的部份──我的靈魂。
我的靈魂告訴肉體它可以情場獲勝，
而那一塊肉卻急迫地等不及聲明，
一聽到你的名字便昂首指向你，
你是它的戰利品；瞧它躊躇滿志之情，
他多麼樂於做你可憐的奴隸，
挺立於你的宮門，並累倒於你身。
 天地良心，我當無愧地叫它作愛，
 為了她那寶貝，我總是上下升沉。

---

① 良心(conscience)，此處是雙關語。前綴 con 源自拉丁語，對莎士比亞及其同時代人來說，此詩中有 con 作前綴的詞容易使人聯想到女性生殖器。此類巴洛克式的雙關猥褻語，可參看《亨利五世》第五幕第二場 285-321 行。

Sonnet 152

In loving thee thou know'st I am forsworn,
But thou art twice forsworn to me love swearing:
In act thy bed-vow broke, and new faith torn
In vowing new hate after new love bearing.
But why of two oaths' breach do I accuse thee
When I break twenty? I am perjured most,
For all my vows are oaths but to misuse thee,
And all my honest faith in thee is lost.
For I have sworn deep oaths of thy deep kindness,
Oaths of thy love, thy truth, thy constancy ,
And to enlighten thee gave eyes to blindness,
Or made them swear against the thing they see.
For I have sworn thee fair : more perjured eye
To swear against the truth so foul a lie.

152

你知道為了愛你,我背叛了另一個情人,
但你發誓愛我,卻又雙重背信。
你推翻枕前諾,拋棄了新盟誓,
新愛一旦到手,新恨復釀成。
我自己曾毀你二十遭,又何須責你
兩番背盟?我是一貫地毀約成性,
我發盡天下誓,只是為糟蹋你,
我的真情真心全掉進你的真身。
我曾指天發誓,說你溫柔無比,
說你忠心不貳,說你情濃意真,
我不辭雙眼變瞎好使你光彩照人,
或讓眼睛顛倒黑白,說話不講良心。
  我曾發誓說你美,於是更會說謊的眼睛
  便樂於指白為黑,硬把我的謊言證明。

Sonnet 153

Cupid laid by his brand and fell asleep,
A maid of Dian's this advantage found,
And his love-kindling fire did quickly steep
In a cold valley-fountain of that ground,
Which borrowed from this holy fire of Love
A dateless lively heat, still to endure,
And grew a seething bath which yet men prove
Against strange maladies a sovereign cure.
But at my mistress' eye Love's brand new fired,
The boy for trial needs would touch my breast;
I, sick withal, the help of bath desired,
And thither hied, a sad distempered guest,
But found no cure; the bath for my help lies
Where Cupid got new fire: my mistress' eyes.

153 ①

丟下火炬的愛神沉沉入夢鄉，

給月神的使女把良機送上，

她趕緊將逗情激愛之火拾起，

浸入附近的山泉，那泉水冰涼。

既借得這神聖的愛情之火，

這股熱量便不舍晝夜燃燒激盪，

它使流泉如沸水澎湃，有人證明

這溫泉是包治百病的絕妙藥方。

現在愛神又借我情人之眼點燃情火，

為試功效，他用火炬觸我的胸膛，

我於是病了，便向溫泉求救，

我趕到那兒，滿心裡狂躁又悽涼。

　　可溫泉失效；因為它本來自我情人的雙眼，

　　就連愛神的火炬，也不得不由它復燃。

---

① 本首詩與第 154 首被某些莎評家認為與莎士比亞其他十四行詩無關。亦有人認為這只是希臘譯詩。

Sonnet 154

The little love-god lying once asleep
Laid by his side his heart-inflaming brand,
Whilst many nymphs that vowed chaste life to keep
Came tripping by; but in her maiden hand
The fairest votary took up that fire
Which many legions of true hearts had warmed,
And so the general of hot desire
Was sleeping by a virgin hand disarmed.
This brand she quenched in a cool well by,
Which from Love's fire took heat perpetual,
Growing a bath and healthful remedy
For men diseased; but I, my mistress' thrall,
Came there for cure; and this by that I prove:
Love's fire heats water, water cools not love.

154

有一次,小愛神沉沉走入夢鄉,
他那點燃情焰的火炬就放在身旁,
許多發誓長保童貞的仙女這時路過,
其中最美的那個仙女玉手輕揚,
將愛神的火炬偷偷地拿起,
那火炬曾溫暖過千萬人的心房。
可憐這欲望如火的堂堂大將,
卻在夢中被玉女解除了武裝。
她在附近的冷泉裡澆滅了火炬,
於是愛火之熱便永在泉水裡隱藏,
從此溫泉長在,成為治病良方。
因為我的情人使我愁鎖肝腸,
　　我於是到溫泉求治卻悟出了真理:
　　愛火能使水發燙,水卻難使愛火涼

異文

莎士比亞十四行詩第 2 首異文：Spes Altera

莎士比亞十四行詩第 106 首異文：On His Mistress' Beauty

莎士比亞十四行詩第 138 首異文：Untitled

莎士比亞十四行詩第 144 首異文：Untitled

莎士比亞十四行詩集

Sonnet 2

When forty winters shall besiege thy brow
And trench deep furrows in that lovely field,
Thy youth's fair liv'ry, so accounted now,
Shall be like rotten weeds of no worth held.
Then being asked where all thy beauty lies,
Where all the lustre of thy youthful days,
To say 'Within these hollow sunken eyes'
Were an all-eaten truth and worthless praise.
O how much better were thy beauty's use
If thou couldst say 'This pretty child of mine
Saves my account and makes my old excuse',
Making his beauty by succession thine.
This were to be new born when thou art old,
And see thy blood warm when thou feel'st it cold.

Sonnet 106

When in the annals of all-wasting time
I see descriptions of the fairest wights,
And beauty making beautiful old rhyme
In praise of ladies dead and lovely knights;
Then in the blazon of sweet beauty's best,
Of face, of hand, of lip, of eye, of brow,
I see their antique pen would have expressed
E'en such a beauty as you master now.
So all their praises were but prophecies
Of these our days, all you prefiguring,
And for they saw but with divining eyes
They had not skill enough your worth to sing;
For we which now behold these present days
Have eyes to wonder, but no tongues to praise.

莎士比亞十四行詩集

Sonnet 138

When my love swears that she is made of truth
I do believe her though I know she lies,
That she might think me some untutored youth
Unskiful in the world's false forgeries.
Thus vainly thinking that she thinks me young,
Although I know my years be past the best,
I, smiling, credit her false-speaking tongue,
Outfacing faults in love with love's ill rest.
But wherefore says my love that she is young,
And wherefore say not I that I am old?
O, love's best habit's in a soothing tongue,
And age in love loves not to have years told.
Therefore I'll lie with love, and love with me,
Since that our faults in love thus smothered be.

Sonnet 144

Two loves I have, of comfort and despair,
That like two spirits do suggest me still.
My better angel is a man right fair,
My worser spirit a woman coloured ill.
To win me soon to hell my female evil
Tempteth my better angel from my side,
And would corrupt my saint to be a devil,
Wooing his purity with her fair pride;
And whether that my angel be turned fiend,
Suspect I may, yet not directly tell;
For being both to me, both to each friend,
I guess one angel in another's hell.
The truth I shall not know, but live in doubt
Till my bad angel fire my good one out.

莎士比亞十四行詩集

莎士比亞十四行詩用語詞典

　　莎士比亞時代的英語屬於早期現代英語，許多單詞的含義與現當代英詞有頗大的區別，爲了方便學習莎士比亞十四行詩原作或研究英國十六世紀前後英語的學者查閱，我們把出現在莎士比亞十四行詩中那些與現當代英語含義區別較大的單詞，及其較特殊的含義列表如下，並酌情譯成漢語。某些單詞可能還有更多的含義，但是基本上有別於現當代英語的含義絕大多數都已列出來了。讀者在檢索本表所列單詞的時候，還可以參考專門的莎士比亞詞典，更準確地理解、欣賞莎士比亞十四行詩。

A

a（可作爲代詞用）代表熟悉的、不強調的「他」
abhor 厭惡、抗議
abide 期待……的發生；爲……而付罰金
able 爲……擔保、爲……出庭作證
about 不規律的、間接的；正在行動中
abroad 離開，步行，流行的，現在的

abuse 冤枉，不良習慣，欺詐；欺騙，使受辱
accident 現象，事件
achieve 終止，結束，贏得，獲得
acture 行動
addition 傑出的標誌，頭銜
admire 驚訝、驚奇
advantage 機遇，利息；得益
advice 考慮，深謀遠慮
advised 謹愼，知曉，深思熟慮
affection 熱情，欲望，性情，矯揉造作
after 依據……，以……的比率

Shakespeare's Sonnets

against 期待，爲將來做準備，在……時候
aim 目標，猜測
alter 交換
an 如果，雖然，究竟，彷彿
anon 很快，即將到來
appeal 譴責；起訴
approve 證實，顯示……是眞實的，確認，試驗證明有罪
argument 證據，辯論的對象，對象－事件，摘要
aspect 面貌，瞥一眼，行星的位置和影響，景象
assay 審判，努力嘗試
assure 訂婚，轉讓財產
Ate 不幸與毀滅之神
attaint 證明有罪，感染；影響，證明不忠，使蒙羞
aught 任何事物

B

bait 向……放狗，焦慮，迫害，用餌引誘，餵食，盛宴
banquet 甜食，以水果和甜食爲主的淡餐
bases 騎士穿的裙式外套
bastard 西班牙甜酒

bent 傾向，方向，緊張，力量，範圍，目標
blazon 族徽，描述，宣佈；公佈，讚揚
blow 膨脹，開花，（蒼蠅）產卵（在）……，弄髒
boot 戰利品，獲利，有利，幫助，利用，有利於，增加；有用
brave 穿著講究的，華麗的，優秀的；虛張聲勢或威脅；喜愛，挑戰，虛張聲勢嚇人，嘲弄
breast 聲音
breathe 說話，鍛鍊，休息
breathed 操練的，英勇的，有靈感的
brief 信，摘要
broke 討價還價
broken （音樂的）片段，不同樂器的樂譜
burn 受性病感染

C

can 知道，對……熟練
carcanet 項鏈
carriage 承受的能力
carve 刺，造型，用表情和姿態邀請
case 陰道

cast 擲骰子，沾染，成立的；拋擲，嘔吐，算帳，推斷，增加
centre 地球或宇宙的中心
certain 固定的
character 寫字、書法、筆跡；寫
cheater 指定去看管被國王沒收財產的官員
child 小女孩，出生高貴的青年
civil 城市的，有秩序的
clerk 學者
closure 領域，範圍，圍起，結論
colour 藉口，託辭
complexion 身體習慣或體格，氣質，外觀，面色
composition 一貫，達成一致
conceit 主意，計畫，憂慮，理解，判決，聯想，想像瑣碎之事；想，估計，預測
conceited 充滿幻想的，有發明才能的，有某種想法的
conscience 知識，理解，顧慮
contain 保持
convert 旋轉，改變
copy 原本的；客觀事物，土地所有權的保有（期限）
counsel 祕密的，祕密的目的或想法
credent 相信，可信的
credit 信譽，名譽，名望

cry 一群豬狗；循氣味方向吠叫
cunning 知識，技能；天才
Cupid 愛神邱比特，維納斯和戰神的兒子，通常被認為是一個佩戴弓箭的小男孩
curious 焦急的，缺乏照顧的，吹毛求疵的，難以取悅的，精緻的，製造精美的；優美地，微妙地
cut 閹割的馬；陰門

D

dazzle 耀眼，炫目的強光
date 時間，期限，生命的期限，結束，末日
dear 重要的，具有能量的，可怕的
defeat 毀滅；損傷外貌，詐騙
derive 繼承，傳下，招致（懲罰等），拖拉
determinate 使穩固；終結，決然的，有意的，已訂婚的
determination 終止，決定，意圖
discourse 推論，談話，交談的力量，熟悉
disease 麻煩，懊惱；擾亂
dismount 放低、降下，從鞘中拔出
distract 分隔，使困窘，使瘋狂

do 與……交媾
doom 判決
double 虛假，欺騙；幽靈
doubt 嫌疑，恐懼；懷疑，懼怕
draw 撤出，騰空，尋求遊戲，循氣息追蹤
dressing 整修，潤飾
dun 黑的；褐色的馬

E

eager 酸（味）的，苦（味）的
ear 耕，用力掘
ecstasy 激動，暈厥狀態，瘋狂
edge 食欲，欲望
eisel 醋
ensconce 隱蔽，躲藏
envy 惡意，敵意；對……表示惡意
erst 從前
estimate 評論，價值，名望
expiate 終結
extend 極度讚揚，誇大價值，以武力強佔

F

face 外表，正義的外表；偽裝，英勇的，華麗的，暴漢，欺凌弱小者，厚臉皮的，整齊

faculty 氣質，品德
fading 一首歌的疊句
fairing 天賦的才能，禮物
fame 謠言，傳聞，名譽；使出名
familiar 隨行的精靈或精神
fancy 愛情，異想天開；愛（某人），墜入愛河
fangled 浮華的
fault 缺少，（打獵時）獸跡中斷
favour 仁慈，惠贈之物，徽章，魅力，外表，臉
feat 機巧的，優雅的；行為
feature 容貌特徵，外形，形狀，清秀
feed 草地，牧場
fee-simple 永遠屬於擁有者及其繼承人的地產，絕對擁有的屬地
fell 粗暴的，殘酷的，憤怒的；皮膚，羊毛或頭髮的表層，羊毛
fight 海戰中保護海員的屏障
fill 履行
fine 完結，終；使結束，支付，按可付金額支付，處罰
flesh 以流血的方式進入、創始、傳授祕訣，使激動、變紅，使滿足
flourish 虛飾，裝飾，華美的裝飾
fanfare of trumpets 嘹亮的喇叭聲

foison 收穫，莊稼豐收
fond 愚蠢的，傻的，瑣碎的，渴望的
fool 職業性的小丑，表愛意或憐憫的用語，玩具
forbid 被咒的
formal 傳統的，威嚴的，心智健全的
former 最初的
forsake 拒絕，不予理會，否認
frame 發明，構造，計畫；準備，使……發生，實行
frank 放縱的，大方的，無拘束的；豬圈；關入欄內
free 大方的，度量大的，天眞無邪的人，無煩惱的；赦免，放逐
frequent 沉溺於某種嗜好中的，熟悉的
friend 情人、情婦
front 前額，臉，戰鬥最前方，開始；面臨，對抗
fury 發怒，熱情，詩的激情，復仇女神

G

gentle 出身高貴的；使尊貴
glance 暗示，對……表輕蔑
glass 鏡子，沙漏

good 金錢上有保障，富有
grow 到期的，應付的
guard 警戒，邊界，整修；裝飾
gust 喜好，滋味

H

habit 服裝，外表
habitude 氣質，脾氣
hair 和善的，性格
half 伴侶
haply 也許，偶然
head 水中突出的（高）陸地，題目，軍隊
heavy 重要的，沉悶的，遲鈍的，困倦的，悲痛的
Helen 絕色美女，古希臘斯巴達國王的妻子，曾被帕里斯擄到特洛伊
him 公（狗）
hive 蜂巢形帽子
honest 可尊敬的，有道德的，貞潔的
honour 貞節
humour 濕氣；據說由人體內血、痰、膽汁和憂鬱構成的液體，其組成部分的差異決定著人的個體氣質；氣質，心情，突然興起的念頭，任性，傾向

333

Shakespeare's Sonnets

husband 撐持家務的人；耕種，耕耘
husbandry 管理，節儉

I

idle 空虛，微不足道的，無價值的，無用的，愚蠢的，有精神病的
image 相似，摹本，描寫，標誌，賦與形體，觀念
impart 足以承擔，使……知名
import 捲入，暗指，表現，重要的，對……有影響，成為……的前兆
incapable 不能接受或實現
indigest 無定型的，未成形的一團物體
indirectly 不公正地，推諉地，通過暗示，不注意地
influence 稱來自天上的空氣般輕靈的流體，對人的性格及命運能產生影響，靈感
inherit 擁有
injurious 侮辱的，有惡意的
intelligence 音信，見聞，消息，獲得祕密情報，暗探；傳遞情報
interest 公理，頭銜，分享

J

jade 處境惡劣或脾氣暴烈的馬，表示蔑視的詞語；穿舊，愚弄
jealous 多疑的，害怕，擔憂，可疑的
jealousy 懷疑，擔憂，不信任
jet 昂首闊步地走，入侵
jollity 鮮豔服裝
jump 正好，精確地；危險；孤注一擲，一致，巧合
just 眞實的，值得尊敬的，精確的
justify 保持對……的清白，判決，證實，確證

K

kind 自然的，溫柔的，有禮貌的，情深的；自然，手段、方式，種族，種類
knot 設計奇異的花床或花園

L

lace 裝飾
large 大方的，揮霍的，無拘束的，不適當的
latch 攻擊，抓住，獲得，迷惑
laund 林間空地

lay 賭博
learn 教
let 障礙、妨害；節制，原因
level 目標，火線，範圍；瞄準，猜測
lie 寄宿，逗留，安靜，在獄中或取防守的姿勢
like 使高興，情況良好
limit 規定的時間，產後休假，部位；任命
line 等級，赤道，測量用的繩子；與……交媾、結合
linger 延長，延期
list 侷限，境界，用柵欄將斜坡圍起來，想要；討好，寧願
long 原本應在
loose 未縛的，疏忽的；箭離弦的時刻，最後一刻
lose 使滅亡，忘記
lover 朋友，女主人、情婦
lust 快感，欲望
lusty 歡樂的，淫蕩的
luxury 色欲

M

make 成配偶，丈夫或妻子
making 形狀、姿勢，外觀

manner 在小偷身上發現的被竊貨物
map 描繪，體現
Mars 戰神或士兵的保護神
maund 籃子
measure 排場很大的舞蹈；曲調；測量
memory 追悼的，紀念品，紀念
merely 簡單地，整個地
merit 獎勵
methinks 我似乎覺得
minion 最喜愛的，親愛的，妓女，乖巧的動物或人
miser 可憐的人
misprision 輕視，錯誤，誤解
mistake 錯誤地進行或發言，錯判，大錯，對……感到擔憂
modern 每天，普通
modesty 適度，避免誇張
moiety 一半，分享，一小部份
moment 原因
monument 墳墓，雕像，徵兆
mood 氣氛，外表，樣式
mother 歇斯底里
motion 動機，木偶戲，傀儡；求婚
mow 愁眉苦臉
muse 驚訝
mutual 共同的，親密的

Shakespeare's Sonnets

N

naked 徒手的，平凡的
naught 邪惡，邪惡的，毀壞的，毀壞
neglect 疏忽的原因
next 最近的、最快的
nice 任性的，嬌弱的，害羞的，難以討好的，難取悅的，小心翼翼的，精巧的，必需的嚴謹，微妙的平衡，複雜的，絲毫不差的，技術好的，微不足道的
niggard 行事小里小氣，節儉地供應
nothing 女陰，陰門

O

obsequious 守本分的，在舉行葬禮方面盡責
occasion 機會，藉口，理由，事件的經過
o'erlook 審查，施以魔術，蔑視
offend 傷害、損害
office 職務，服務
offices 放家用物品的房間
oppression 負擔，痛苦
orb 圈，範圍，行星運行軌道，天體，地球
outlive 逃……劫難、存活
outward 外表
owe 擁有、佔有

P

pace 訓練（馬）走路
pain 麻煩，處罰
painful 費勁的，勞苦的
pale 柵欄，圍欄，包圍，以環圍繞
paper 公佈罪行的告示；寫下來
part 動作，邊，面
partake 分給，偏袒，與……站在一起
particular 細節，個人，個人利益，親密
personal 有關個人的短聞
passion 苦楚，苦惱，陣發的疾病，強烈的激情，充滿激情的講話，哀傷，深深感覺到的激情
passionate 帶著激情表達；有同情心的，悲傷的
patent 頭銜，特權，當局
patience 允許，許可
pattern 先例，模範；樹立榜樣，成為……的模範和先例
pencil 畫筆

perfect 消息非常靈通的，裝備，準備就緒的；完成，教導
perfection 履行
perspective 產生奇形怪狀形象的一種光學器械，產生變形效果或意外效果的圖像
pervert 轉向
phoenix 一種獨一無二的阿拉伯鳥，此鳥在死亡的時候從自己的骨灰中再生
phraseless 難以表達的
pied 眼色斑駁的
pleasant 歡樂的，使人發笑的
plight 保證、誓約
point 最高點，結論，句號
policy 政府，當局，在管理公私事務時的小心謹慎，狡猾，詭詐，奸計
politic 與政府和當局打交道，狡詐
pomp 行列，盛會
posied 刻上一句箴言
potential 強有力的
power 軍隊
praise 評價，價值
precedent 前者；供摹仿的原作，符號
prefer 呈遞，建議，介紹，推薦
presage 預兆，預知

presence 寢室，朋友，傢伙，人
present 立刻的，馬上；現金，展示、呈遞或提供反對某人的控訴
press 人群，印刷、出版，食櫥，徵兵的當局；強制地；擁擠，壓迫，強迫服兵役
prevent 預期，逃跑，避免
pride 堂皇，盛飾；最高狀態，勇氣，性欲
prime 首先的，主要的、領導的，煽起性欲；春天的時光
private 私人
prize 競爭；估價，尊重
prone 準備就緒的，熱衷的
proof 考試，考驗，經驗，爭論點，結果
proud 興高采烈的，說出自豪的理由，高尚的，美妙的，有精神的，過分繁茂的，煽起性欲
prove 嘗試，考驗，通過經驗找到，經驗
publish 使眾所周知，正式宣佈，攻擊
purpose 求婚、申請，談話

Q

qualify 使緩和,減輕,平息,克制,加水沖淡
quality 成就,官階,專業,朋黨,特色,原因
quest 評審團,審訊,調查團體
quick 流動的,新鮮的,無耐性的
quietus 清帳
quit 釋放,使除去,宣告無罪,使自己被宣告無罪,使自己清帳,報仇,償還,報復、報答

R

race 姜根(精力的根源),血統,種屬,天性
rack 驅使雲彩;使受痛苦,伸展,擴張,拉緊
rage 瘋狂,壞脾氣,性激情;使憤怒
rank 生長過度茂盛,長得太胖,難以控制的,高的,好色的,熱情奔放的,粗糙的,生膿;緊密地
raven 貪婪地吞吃
read 教導,發現……的意義,解清謎團
reason 言詞,批評;談論,討論,解釋
receipt 所接受的東西,容器,接受,容量,祕訣
receiving 理解,招待
record 證人,記憶;目睹,唱
region 高空,空氣
rehearse 描述,告訴
religion 嚴厲的忠貞,宗教職責
religious 精確的,有良心的,嚴謹的
remember 提到,紀念,提醒
removed 遙遠的,隱居的,為時空所隔離
remover 改變者
render 投降,還帳,陳述;給回,照實描述,宣佈,述說,屈服
repair 恢復的,來的;去,來,回歸
replication 回答,回聲
respect 關係,歧視,考慮,尊重;尊敬,關心
rest 休息的地方,恢復力氣,決議,後備賭資
resty 難以駕馭的,懶惰的
retention 居留,貯存,保有……的實力
revolt 嫌惡,變化;反叛

revolution 變更,時間造成的變化
rim 如肚狀的部份,腹,墊在腹部的膜狀物
riot 放蕩的生活,放蕩
rondure 圈,圓
rude 無知的,野蠻的,暴力的,粗糙的東西或狀況
rudeness 暴力,粗暴
ruffle 喧鬧;虛張聲勢嚇人,盛氣凌人,擺架子,狂暴的

S

sable 黑色
sad 堅定的,墓地,嚴肅的,沮喪
sadly 陰鬱的,嚴肅的
saucy 自傲的,放肆的,任性的
savour 氣味,芳香,風格,品格
saw 格言,箴言,諺語
say 精織成的布,滋味,格言
scale 手段,路,方式
scape 任意妄為,違法;逃跑
scope 目的地,目標,目的,主題,無禮,自由
score 贏得,得分,用刻痕計算,刻痕
scorn 辱罵,侮辱,受到輕蔑的對象
seeing 外表

seen 熟練的、有技術的
self 自我的,同樣的
sense 生理感覺,官能,性欲,精神憂慮,心靈,意見
sequent 繼續的,後來的
service 放在桌面上吃的東西
several 明晰的,不同的,個體的,分別的,各式各樣的
shadow 使陰暗;躲藏,庇護
sheaved 用稻草造的
siege 破產,官階,糞(塊)
sight 面具,面頰
sightless 看不見的,醜陋的
simple 草藥,某種混合物中的單一成分
simplicity 無知,愚蠢
single 輕微的,微不足道的,誠摯的,簡樸的
size 津貼
skill 判斷,推理,能力;造成區別,有重要性
slave 使成為奴隸,使卑躬屈膝
sleided 繭絲,使鬆開成細線
smother 令人窒息的煙
sole 獨一無二的,純粹的,單獨的
sometime 曾經,從前

Shakespeare's Sonnets

sort 一組,等級,朋友,群,方式,身分,狀態;分配,規定,結果……是,適合的,相適應,使適合,合宜,分類,想要,發明,有人陪伴著去
sound 十足的,聲明,保持完善
speed 氣運,結果,保護,幫助;生活得(好或壞),結果……是,成功的,支持,寵愛
spend 消費,消耗盡
spoil 掠奪,掠奪物,毀壞;搶奪,奪取
spot 玷辱,恥辱,鑲邊的圖案
spring 噴泉,來源,草木的枝條
stain 沾染,使失色,變暗淡,模糊的
stale 引誘人或物,誘餌,妓女,笑柄,馬尿
stamp 蓋印的工具,硬幣,勳章,表示傑出的標誌,蓋印於;使獲得印象,打上記號,批准
stand 某人埋伏的地方;面對,對抗,森嚴壁壘地對抗
stand on 堅持,依靠,倚靠,對……有影響,……的職責或利益
stand to 勃起,支撐,維持,堅持
stand to it 維持一個事業,採取立場

state 情形,健康或繁盛狀態,等級,尊嚴,王位,貴族,統治集團,政府
statute 契約,抵押
stay 障礙;扣留,站立,挺立等候,伺奉
stern 掌舵者
stick 刺,拴住或固定住,遲疑
still 總是,持續不斷地
sting 性欲
stone 鏡子,晴天霹靂,睪丸;變成石頭
stop 風琴竅,停止在音調上產生差別,音樂和弦指法
staunch 堅固的,治癒
store 培育,增長;使人民居住
stout 大膽,強壯,驕傲的
strain 種族,性格,和善的,階級,曲調;鉤子,力量,束縛,激勵
strange 外國的,新的,不知道,不友好的,冷淡的,害羞的
strangely 冷漠地,不打招呼,作爲一個陌生人,到達一個非同尋常的程度,以不同尋常的方式
straw 小把稻草,恥辱的標記
strength 權威、當局,合法權力,部隊
style 頭銜

340

subjection 臣民的或作爲臣民的職責
subtle 薄的，細微的，狡猾的，不忠義的，狡猾
succession 緊跟，繼承人，成功
successive 世襲的，代代相傳的
sufferance 苦楚，損害，忍耐
suggest 誘使，誘使變壞，暗示
suppose 假定，指望；相信，想像，猜測
sure 安全的，可靠的，團結的
surety 確信安全，確實，穩定，擔保
suspect 猜疑
swart 黑暗的，黑黝黝的
sway 方向，控制，主權；統治，使移動
swear 發誓，作僞誓
sweet 有香味的；氣味

T

table 碑銘，書寫板，可以畫畫的平面，手掌主紋之間的矩形空間
tables 西洋雙陸棋戰
take 打擊，使用疾病或魔法打擊，抓住，產生效果，推斷，測量，寫下，信以爲眞，著火，領會，理解，尊敬，取走，下結論；帶頭，偏離，出軌

take in 抓住
take me with you 請說得讓我能聽懂
take it on 弄權
take on 發怒，顯示很大的苦惱，假裝
take out 抄一遍，留副本
take up lift 使服兵役，協助，逮捕，賒購，嚴厲指責，譴責，反對，遭遇
tale 逐一編號，談話，故事，虛構之事物
tall 長的，高尚的，優秀的，美好的，勇敢的
'tame 給（一個木桶）鑽孔
task 租稅，把任務強加給，佔據，使……緊張，驗證
teen 苦惱，悲哀，哀傷
tell 認爲，計數
temperate 貞潔的，俗世的
tempt 考驗，冒險
tend 聽，留心，伺奉，等
tender 提供，提供的東西，小心；顯示，喜歡；有同情心的
termless 難以形容的
text 大寫字母
thing 性器官
think 似乎
thought 焦慮，憂傷
thriftless 無利益可得的

tis 這（方言的）
to 加之，相反，適宜於，較之，就……，至於
toil 網，陷阱；使努力工作，倦於工作
top 頭，額髮，最高點；與……結合、交媾
touch 試金石，污點；試探，考驗，傷口
tract 追蹤，蹤跡，所經之路線
trade 來來往往，道路，習慣，商務
transfix 移動
translate 改變，使變形
trench 砍
triumph 公眾慶典，王牌
triumphant 凱旋式的，慶祝勝利
troth 眞理，信仰
try 考驗；使潔淨，精鍊，查驗
twire 閃爍
tyranny 暴力，暴虐
tyrant 篡權者

U

undertake 負責，擔任，與……有關，冒險
unexperient 沒有經驗的
unfair 偷盜美

unhappily 不適宜地
unkind 不自然的
untainted 沒有受到指控的
untrimmed 裸體的
up 武裝起來，起義；上上下下，完全地，精確地
upon 由於，有鑒於
use 習慣，風俗，一般性經驗，優點，利益，放債收利，借出之物的利潤，需要；習慣，繼續，實際做（某事），對付，處理，常去

V

vantage 利益，利潤，優勢，據點、有利地位，機會
vaunt 開始
vice 在道德劇中代表一種惡的人物，小丑，滑稽劇演員，用來抓緊物體的工具；用螺絲釘釘上
virtue 勇氣，優點，成就，能力，功效，實質
virtuous 強有力的，有益的
voice 言辭，話，謠言，傳聞，表達出來的意見，判斷，投票，贊同，將要聽到的權威的話；歡呼

vulgar 俗人的，人盡皆知的，普通的，公眾的，平庸的；普通人，白話

W

wake 一直醒著，由於狂歡或守衛而熬到夜深，因缺乏睡眠而精疲力竭，喚醒
walk 森林中的寬闊地面
want 缺乏、錯失
wanton 嬉戲的，難管訓的，反覆無常的，奢侈的，華美的，好色的，不貞潔的；寵壞了的孩子，受溺愛的寵兒（戀人等），無賴的，娛樂的，難以駕馭或淫蕩的人
ward 警衛，監視，牢房，在擊劍中採取守勢；保護
waste 花費，浪費
watch 警醒狀態，不眠狀態，警覺性；醒著，一直不睡覺，當場捉獲
water 光澤

wear 流行；舉止，纏住，時髦的，使人厭倦的
weed 衣服的一件，衣服
where 而
wide 失去記號，迷途的
wild 魯莽的，意亂情迷的，自由進出的
will 男（女）性器官
wink 睡眠，閉眼
wit 精神力量，心靈，感覺，智慧，想像，有這類特點的人；體會
withal 與……一道，及，同時，和
without 超過，遠離，在……之外
wonder 欽佩；對……感驚奇
wood 發瘋的
world 結婚；已婚婦女
worship 威嚴，名譽，權力，權威；使……榮耀
worthy 出色的，有價值的，應得的，根基堅實的，適合的
wrack 毀壞
writ 文件，寫成之文件，委任統治權，書面指令，《聖經》（的一節）

好站連結

Project Gutenberg
Michael Hart 發起的「古騰堡計劃」。1971 年開始將公共版權圖書數位化，目前有數萬本書可免費下載
http://www.gutenberg.org

The Oxford Text Archive
原始「牛津全文檔案室」。收集、校訂、建立可靠的資料庫，推廣電子全文在學術社群中的使用 http://ota.bodleian.ox.ac.uk

Shakespeare's Sonnets
莎氏十四行詩主題網站。提供莎詩原始版本，每詩皆附翻譯、注釋與評析；亦提供莎士比亞同時代詩人的作品
http://www.shakespeares-sonnets.com

The Internet Shakespeare Editions
加拿大維多利亞大學 (University of Victoria) 英語系的莎學研究網站。點選「The Library」可瀏覽高解析度的 1609 年莎氏十四行詩四開本 (Quarto) 和其他十七世紀出版的莎作對開本 (Folio)
http://www.uvic.ca

Shakespeare Study guide
自由作家 Michael J. Cummings 的個人網站。提供莎詩導讀與世界文學評論
http://www.cummingsstudyguides.net

Sonnet Central
收錄英美十四行詩經典作品,並節選世界各國大師名作
http://www.sonnets.org

The Shakespeare Institute
英國伯明罕大學 (University of Birmingham) 莎士比亞研究所。提供莎學研究、教學與英國文藝復興時期文化史碩士學程
http://www.birmingham.ac.uk

The Shakespeare Institute Library, University of Birmingham
莎士比亞研究所附設圖書館。典藏主題為莎學與英國文藝復興時期文學相關文獻
https://www.birmingham.ac.uk/facilities/sil

The Folger Shakespeare Library
美國華府 (Washington, D.C.) 的福爾傑莎士比亞圖書館暨文藝復興時期研究中心。典藏主題含括莎士比亞同時代作家、伊莉莎白時代的社會與文化
http://www.folger.edu

Shakespeare's Birthplace Trust
莎翁故居、博物館、莎士比亞中心圖書館 (The Shakespeare Centre Library in Stratford-upon-Avon)。圖書館彙整了莎翁故居信託管理局 (Shakespeare's Birthplace Trust) 與皇家莎翁劇團 (Royal Shakespeare Company) 的典藏文獻;與莎士比亞研究所附設圖書館、福爾傑莎士比亞圖書館並列為三大莎學圖書館
http://www.shakespeare.org.uk

The World Shakespeare Bibliography Online
福爾傑莎士比亞圖書館與霍普金斯大學出版社 (The Johns Hopkins University Press) 合作，提供 1963 年迄今的莎學研究文獻連結。須註冊與付費
http://www.worldshakesbib.org

Shakespeare Online
莎士比亞與文藝復興時期研究者 Amanda Mabillard 的個人網站。提供莎士比亞研究與教學資訊，含文學理論、批評與學術期刊的分類索引
http://www.shakespeare-online.com

The British Shakespeare Association
英國莎士比亞協會。提供各種莎學研討會、演出資訊、劇評與新聞
http://www.britishshakespeare.ws

The Shakespeare Association of America
美國莎士比亞協會。致力於推廣莎學研究與教學，並提供獎學金
http://www.shakespeareassociation.org